MISSING LOVE

ELITE MEN OF MANHATTAN BOOK 4

MISSY WALKER

BLURB

Olivia

I'd been handed the contract of a lifetime, revamping the flagship Madison Avenue store of Fashion icon, Farrah Goldsmith Couture.

There was only one person standing in my way.

Her grandson, Ari. Sorry, Aristotle, as he liked to remind me.

Self-righteous and a pompous jerk, he was my arch-enemy and now my boss.

I wanted him to get hit by a bus or run over by a pack of rhinos. But no, I wasn't that lucky.

For the next three weeks, I'm stuck with him and his sickly gorgeous body and mocha-colored eyes.

Help.

Ari

She thought I was an arrogant jerk... I thought she was uptight and sassy.

I didn't like her before, but now that I was her boss, I had the upper hand.

So making her life a living hell was priority number one... until it wasn't.

I don't understand why she ignites a fire inside me. All I knew was I was addicted hook, line, and sinker.

Now, if only she'd let me in.

An enemies-to-lovers steamy boss romance with a HEA that will leave you swooning.

Trigger warning - Scenes of loss are part of this novel.

Copyright © 2022 by Missy Walker

All rights reserved.

No part of this publication may be reproduced, distributed or transmitted in any form or by any means, including by any electronic or mechanical means, including photocopying, recording or information storage and retrieval systems, without prior written consent from the author, except for the use of brief quotations in a book review.

Cover Design: Missy Walker

Editor: Swish Design & Editing

To my fans. Without you, I couldn't do what I love to do every single day. Thank you so much for your endless support. It truly means the world to me x

PROLOGUE
ARI

I tossed my beer back. Ice-cold and crisp, it cooled the back of my throat, but it did little to quell the frustration brewing in my chest. Olivia, the blonde-haired woman, reared up at me like a python ready to strike.

"Could you two honestly stop bickering!" Lourde intervened, pulling her fiancé close, frustrated like the rest of our friends at the constant back and forth between Olivia and me. It wasn't my fault the woman was seriously painful and sassy and has had it out for me since we met a few months back via mutual friends.

"Honestly, guys, we are all getting sick of your squabbling," Pepper added.

I took my stare away from the ashy blonde, blue-eyed monster opposite to take in our friends. They all nodded in agreement, frustrated with our constant disagreements. The truth was, our debates were rather heated at times, and clearly, we had different points of view on most things.

"What was the argument about last time?" Pepper asked, shaking her head at the memory.

"Mr. Rich Kid over there was razzing me over the benefits

of overseas labor." Olivia folded her arms across her chest and gritted her perfect teeth. Her response was so quick I wondered if she'd been ruminating on it since we last saw each other.

My gaze drifted to her cleavage. She had a nice rack, but she may as well have a tattoo on her forehead that said *fuck off* with that fiery mouth because no man would ever touch her.

"I, for one, think I'm thoroughly entertained by you both." Connor let out a laugh, and his girlfriend, Pepper, shot him dagger eyes.

I let out a chuckle, then took another sip as Olivia held my gaze, a fury burning in the depths. If I wasn't laughing at our interaction, I was furious—it was a fine line, and right now, I wasn't sure which way I would tip.

"Tell Miss Know-It-All over there then that I've never roofied any woman before to get laid."

Lourde laughed aloud, followed by cackles of laughter around the table. "Olivia, come on, you didn't say that, did you?"

"I wouldn't put it past him. He's so arrogant and full of himself. He wouldn't know what to do if a woman ever turned him down."

"Never happened, sweetheart, and never will." My gaze fell to my crotch. "Believe the rumors, hun. They're all true. I don't need any help in that department." I couldn't resist pressing the matter. It seemed I liked playing with fire.

Olivia rolled her eyes in disgust. "Oh God, let me guess, ten inches of pure thrusting power." Her sarcastic tone wasn't lost on me, but instead of ignoring it, I pushed it further.

Winking at her with a smirk, I lowered my voice as I said, "Thick all the way around too, not like little limp dicks you're probably used to."

Her mouth tipped open, but nothing came out.

"Ari, stop!" Lourde pleaded. Maybe that was a little crass,

but this woman riled me up to that point. I didn't know what would come out of my mouth next.

"Can we not talk about my Ari's dick size? I'm eating a pig in a blanket, for fuck's sake!" Barrett scoffed, looking sideways at his sausage in pastry.

"Arrogant jerk, probably just lies there, expecting her to do all the work… dick, all right."

She turned to me, her lips curling at the corners.

Again, this devil of a woman was goading me.

Barrett cleared his throat, putting a stop to the back and forth for now, and held up his whiskey tumbler. "Cheers to my gorgeous fiancé and Olivia for starting Bespoke Interiors."

We sat around Lourde's living room in Tribeca, drinking to their new success, while other people drunk-danced around us. We were toasting to a new interior design business with her and her pain-in-the-ass friend, Olivia.

Olivia cast her eyes over to Barrett, her scowl immediately lifting into a smile when her eyes disengaged from mine.

We all clicked glasses, and when Olivia and I were the last to toast, I held my glass out, waiting for her. Reluctantly, she held hers close to mine. Then I made an effort to forcefully bump her glass, spilling her drink down her fingers.

"Asshole!" She breathed out a huff of irritation, flicking her hand free of the spilled champagne.

"You guys just need to fuck and move on," Magnus said, finally joining the group after flirting up a storm with a woman nearby.

"Oh my God, never in a million years would I ever…" She wiped her hands with the nearby dishtowel. "I'd rather rub onions in my eyes with Tabasco sauce."

For a moment, I was speechless but quickly recovered not to be outplayed. "I'm sure that can be arranged," I said, topping up my drink, then tipping it back until I emptied it completely.

"Ah, you guys," Pepper remarked and dragged Connor up, heading over to the dance floor, begging to form in Lourde's living room.

Lourde whispered something in Olivia's ear, and she let out a reluctant sigh.

Finally, the alcohol was kicking in, and Lourde's dance floor was heaving with bodies moving and grinding to the DJ's music.

Magnus was sucking face with a woman who looked like she had just stepped out of a strip club, so I was tapping my feet, half listening to Tori talk about her recent photo shoot. When the crowd parted, familiar blonde hair caught my attention.

Olivia came into view. With eyes closed, she ran her hand down her powder blue dress. Curious, I tipped my head to the side, taking her in. If only she was this placid all the time because damn, the woman was seriously gorgeous. A guy started to dance around her, and suddenly my tapping foot hit the ground. Abruptly I stood, finding my way toward the dance floor.

Diverting my attention to Magnus, I yelled in his direction, "I'll be right back." He stopped exploring the surfaces of her face and found me. Then I jerked my head in Tori's direction, and he nodded, knowing exactly what to do. Since Connor and Barrett were taken, Magnus and I were each other's wingmen, so he knew what I needed and when and vice versa without verbally expressing it. He garnered Tori's attention, pulling her into conversation while I took the opportunity to make my way toward the sassy blonde, who held my attention.

Slightly unsteady on my feet, I approached Olivia, watching her dance with a steady gait.

Without thinking, I stepped forward, wrapping an arm around her waist. Immediately, she opened her eyes and gazed up at me through long lashes.

"What do you think you are doing, Ari?" She fumed, but to my surprise, didn't jerk back.

"I don't want some dick taking advantage of you, when you're clearly drunk." I stared down at her, lazy eyes stared back.

"So, you'd prefer to take advantage of me instead?"

Cradling her with my other hand, I wrapped it around her waist and pulled her close. "Whatever you want, sweetheart."

With half-hooded eyes, I shifted my gaze to her lips. She bit her lower lip and turned around her slender back, nestling against my chest. The music slowed down, and her movements turned seductive as she ground against me. I lowered my mouth to her ear. "You're drunk," I whispered. Hitting my senses was a fruity concoction of sweetness that made my dick swell against my seam.

"Finally, we agree on something," she said, taking her hands above her head and sliding them down her body. Pushing her pert ass on my crotch, she teased me, and I sucked in a rampant breath. Before saying anything, I swallowed, knowing my voice was becoming thick with desire. Immediately, my hands slid down the sides of her dress. When she tilted her head back, exposing the column of her neck, I was at a loss for words.

Fuck it.

It was too much for me to ignore in my state. She was too unguarded not to devour. I leaned down, running my lips along her neck, and nipped at her soft skin. Needing more, I spun her around, taking her face between my hands. I pulled her so close she was only a breath away. Finding my voice, I ordered, "No more games, Olivia." My mouth landed on hers, and her pillowy lips opened for me. I kissed her with a force I didn't know I had. Our teeth clashed and tongues intertwined. Her fingernails dug into my arms, and I pulled her closer, her breasts firm against my chest. She tasted of fruit and champagne, and my dick wanted more. A high-pitched sound made Olivia pull back.

"Ari!"

Breathless, Olivia stared at me in shock. She took her hands to her swollen lips in disbelief. I ignored the intrusion, but Olivia didn't. She turned to an awaiting Tori with her hands on her hips and a scowl the size of Everest.

Fuck sake. Great timing.

She stepped back, taking her hand to her head. "Oh my God, what have I done?"

"Nothing you didn't want. Besides, Tori and I aren't together," I said, trying to ignore the interruption standing with her hands on her hips.

Tori, let out an audible huff, scowled, then walked away toward Magnus.

I shrugged. "What? It's true," I said, honestly. Stepping forward, I closed the gap between us, needing more of her. "Where were we?"

She held her hand up, and it landed on my chest. "Don't come near me, Ari…" The force of her words stopped me in my tracks. "Ever again."

1

OLIVIA

I loathed him.

No, strike that, I despised him.

Whenever he was near, the hairs on my neck stood at attention. In the short time I'd known Ari Goldsmith, every conversation we had turned into a battle of wills. A seemingly innocent discussion turned into an argument and one that he enjoyed, which just riled me up that much more.

We didn't see eye to eye on anything, which was completely fine until recently. Mixing in the same friendship circles and seeing him socially, I could barely tolerate it, but now, it was worse.

So much worse.

Now, he was my boss.

The thought made me very uncomfortable. That and the fact I'd kissed him back at Lourde's party last week at a moment when my defenses were down from copious amounts of alcohol and never mind that I had liked it. So much so that if we hadn't been interrupted by one of his model things, I can't exactly say with confidence, things would have stopped then.

Nevertheless, I sat glued to my plastic seat, staring vacantly through the crowd of people, focusing on the slither of darkness in the subway tunnel rather than the desire-laced kiss my arch-enemy had laid upon me.

When I saved Ari's grandmother from a spectacular fall at her fashion show, the last thing I expected was for us to hit it off and for her to hire me. But turning down the opportunity to revamp fashion tycoon Farrah Goldsmith's flagship Manhattan store and potentially those along the East Coast was like shooting yourself in the foot twice. I'd have to be bird-brained to turn the queen of fashion down and rightly so. It was the gift of a lifetime and one I was going to seize with open arms.

There was just one problem standing in my way.

Ari.

Manhattan's famous womanizer and grandson of Farrah Goldsmith had an arrogance that matched his impossibly tall stature. Sickly gorgeous with mocha eyes, thick chestnut hair that swooped perfectly to the tops of his ears, and a chiseled jaw sharp enough to cut glass, he wore a dusting of dark stubble, perfectly kept and groomed just like the women he was with. The same harem of women who worshiped the ground he walked upon, and he, in turn, walked all over them.

Okay, so maybe I googled him after meeting him a few weeks back. Who wouldn't look up a guy you had a fiery debate with over labor wages? That was our first argument, and it left me reeling to the point where I couldn't sleep and ruminated for hours after.

That and how he talked about women like he had bedded the entire town. With broad shoulders atop his six-foot-four muscular frame, he looked like he was carved from granite and should strut the catwalks of New York and Milan alongside his model friends on the runway. Supermodels, Victoria's Secret angels, and celebrities were his M.O. I knew his type. I'd been with enough players to know exactly his type. Heck, I was a player myself. But that didn't bother me as much as his general know-it-all attitude, and at the last meeting, when he called my interior work 'plain,' I wanted to reach across the table and slap him with a Thor-like fist. Knock those perfect teeth straight out. I let out a sigh.

I guarantee his spoiled ass had never had to work a day in his life. He didn't have to wonder where his next meal was coming from, if he was going to eat the next day, if the heating would be shut off, or if he would be evicted, *again*.

Ari, who had no regard for anyone, was my boss.

Mine alone. My business partner, Lourde Diamond, was super busy planning her wedding to Barrett Black and training up the new replacement at Barrett's construction company which we both left to start our own interior design company. So, sigh. I'd taken the lead on this contract.

It was amazing. I couldn't be more thrilled until I found out who I was reporting to. Insert eye roll here and panic attack. It all happened in a whirlwind too. One minute, I was working with Barrett, and the next, I was here doing my thing with Barrett's support.

For the last seven years, I couldn't have asked for a better boss—supportive but firm, two traits I admired and respected. Barrett trusted me with the luxury detail of his house and apartment developments, and I delivered.

So very different from the email I received from my soon-to-be boss. One etched in my brain like a worn tattoo on aged skin.

Ms. Willows,

Farrah has informed me of your new contract with Farrah Goldsmith Couture. How thrilling.

I know my grandmother was taken with you, but you work for me now and therefore you will need to prove yourself. As such, we will be working closely together so I can ensure you meet the highest standards that we expect here at FGC.

Monday morning at eight o'clock we begin. Don't be late.

Your boss.

Aristotle
Vice President
Farrah Goldsmith Couture

And the Asshole of the Year Award goes to…

I mean, seriously, who would send an email like that? How unprofessional, for a start. But I guess Mr. Big Dick could just swing his dick around because he owned the place.

Hmm. If the rumors were true, Ari had a humongous dick.

I shook my head and adjusted in my seat, my shoulder and neck stiff like bricks from the balled-up tension I held the entire subway ride from Williamsburg to Manhattan.

Lowering my head to my left shoulder, I stretched out the tension, then did the same on the right, dipping my head low. Then I rotated my head in slow motion, like a spinning top, feeling it click after a full rotation.

Damn, that feels better.

My gaze settled to the front of the car where a tall man in his mid-twenties, hair slicked back in an ill-fitting suit, was staring me down. A slight grin on his lips formed when our eyes connected.

Cute. Any other day, perhaps we could have a night of fun. It had been a while. I smiled back before my attention once again drifted to the monstrous task ahead of me and the roadblock standing in my way.

The repeated clang of the subway slowed down to a near halt, and a piercing voice came over the speakers. "Lexington Ave," echoed throughout the train.

Picking the invisible lint off my fitted black skirt, I pulled up my tan briefcase resting against my patent black Mary Janes. Then I shuffled my way through the crowded train that smelled like sardines and terrible body odor, clutching the important bag with me. Although worn, with frayed edges and discoloration at the base, it was a briefcase I treasured, bought with my generous bonus from Barrett in the early years I worked for him. Back then, it cost more than a month's salary, and I had plenty to spare. Money that was so life-changing. It gave me the freedom to move out of my rodent-infested apartment in the Bronx and into a shared flat in Williamsburg with my friend and sommelier, Dario Dash.

Damn, Dario. Lucky bastard flew to Italy yesterday on a viticulture experience that would take him to the southern tip of the boot to Sicily and finish up in the Tuscan countryside.

Argh, to have a holiday and feel the Tuscan heat at my back. My blonde bob swishing around my face while I drink a Chianti and smell the Italian pizza in the wood-fired oven, crust bubbling, cheese melting. Maybe one day, I'd afford myself such a trip.

The screech of the train breaks pulled me from my momentary bliss. And my reality smacked me in the face as I stood, seeing my reflection in the glass carriage door as the train came to a sudden jolt. Overpowering cheap perfume, mixed with body odor and dirty laundry, that was my reality and the smelly trip into the city I'd been doing for years.

I chewed the inside of my cheek as uncertainty plagued me. *What was I doing?* I'd given up the job of my dreams to risk the unfamiliar.

Starting my company with Lourde wasn't the daunting

part. It was Ari's lion den, I feared, that was awaiting me in less than ten minutes.

"Hey." A silvery voice pulled my attention.

I turned around to find the handsome man from before standing behind me, his suit brushing up against me. His suit was so ill-fitting from this close that it hurt. How could he not realize it was two sizes too big? Did he still think he had some growing to do?

I smiled at his pleasant tone and waited for the doors to open. "Hey, yourself." I remained beside him, making no move to back away from his advances.

His mouth split into a smile. "They call me Bud." His hand disappeared into his suit jacket pocket.

"You can't get them to stop?" I twisted my lips into a smile.

He snorted out a laugh. "Call me sometime." He pulled a business card from his suit jacket, and I was tempted to recommend an excellent tailor but decided against it.

"Sure." I took the card from his fingers, and at the same time, the doors sprung open. I tucked it into my coat pocket and gripped my briefcase.

His eyes hovered over my glossy red lips. "Till then."

Turning, I walked out with the thousands who departed the train like a swarm of worker bees.

With a renewed spring in my step—thanks to Bud—I remembered why I was here. My grit, skill, and determination. I was a fighter and that snippet of flirting gave me the confidence boost I needed to get out of my head and on with the job at hand. I wouldn't let Ari undermine that, and I wouldn't stand for it because there was no way I was going back to my roots. My poverty-stricken roots. This was the job that was going to put me on the map, and there was nothing or no one that could stand in my way.

Especially Ari.

2

ARI

The elevator doors opened, and I floated onto the sixth and top floor of Farrah headquarters, elated to be back. Immediately, I felt at home. It was as though everything clicked into place and this was where I ought to be. My one-year sojourn ended up close to a decade, and before I knew it, my thirties rolled around, and I was still fucking women like they were on the extinction list.

Partying hard and living off my inheritance was my life. And I fucking loved it. That was until it got boring and every woman wanted me for my last name and my eight-inch cock. Yeah, motherfucker, believe the rumors. They're all true.

I strolled the checkered black-and-white tiled floor offices, the familiar perfume of models infiltrating my senses and a permanent fixture in the executive reception along with my bed.

All four-hundred staff housed in a stunning art deco building my grandmama bought with every cent she had as a single, thirty-five-year-old woman in 1971. A huge investment back then and a gamble, but one that certainly had paid off.

I hadn't taken a trip down to the other five floors. That

would have to wait until after my meeting with the bane-of-my-existence, Ms. Olivia Willows. Being late wasn't an option, but toying with her, well, that I would enjoy, especially since locking lips with the Ice Queen herself.

As a little boy, I spent my school breaks at Farrah headquarters, mesmerized by the intricate detail that went into a couture gown and the huge productions and year-long planning that went into a live fashion show. Yes, Farrah Goldsmith Couture, or FGC as it was often referred to, was my playground, and as soon as I was old enough, Grandmama gave me a job. And so my parents traveled the world, not interested in fashion, and my grandmama showed me the ropes. I had spent more time with her than I did with my own parents in my early twenties. And when everyone was begging me to come out and party, I preferred to sit on the textile floor and learn from the seamstresses or go over the live production schedule with the marketing team just to check the lighting detail was choreographed perfectly for the showstopper gown.

I spent every waking hour here. Who wouldn't? It was a buzz with learning and a supermodel hangout. Models lived and breathed these corridors, regularly getting fitted and measured for upcoming shows and New York Fashion Week.

By the time I was twenty-three, I'd worked my way up through every single floor. Grandmama insisted I learn every little detail of the business to become the vice president of one of the biggest fashion houses in the United States.

Grandmama was constantly in my ear, always wanting me to leave my playboy ways behind to rejoin the family business and, as she put it, get some clarity. But I opted for the lifestyle of Manhattan playboy and hit the social scene burning through my twenties and coasting into my thirties, as a wealthy, bored, and not that I'd admit it to anyone, but a somewhat lonely guy.

"Mr. Goldsmith, so nice to see you again." Carmel smiled

into hollowed cheeks where plump, firm cheeks once belonged. We all age, but I doubted it was from that. Her clothes hung off her like a coat hanger. The amount of weight she dropped was disturbing. In this industry, though, I'd seen it all before.

"Carmel, good to be back," I quipped, pulling my strap up on my shoulder.

"We missed you, *sssir.*" She hissed on the 'S,' blowing out more air than necessary in a purr.

I brushed aside her flirtation and squared my shoulders, ignoring the sultry eyes she cast over me, along with the three other receptionists.

Fucking my way around town was my reputation. But now I had something to prove. I wasn't just a wallet and a handsome face. I was more than that.

I had to be.

I was going to prove to my grandmama that I was the man to take over this place. Not William Sanella, Farrah's right-hand man. There was something not quite right about him, and I couldn't picture him running the business when she retired. If she ever retired. I hoped she wouldn't. The woman was stronger than an ox, but time ended all of our journeys someday, and she was eighty-three now.

I nodded and smiled politely at the heads that turned my way. Gossip was rife here, and by the looks on staff faces, they weren't expecting to see me here today. So, after introducing myself, I promptly left.

Was there no company announcement?

William, considering he was the vice president of Farrah Goldsmith, ought to have sent out a memo. The day-to-day running was on his shoulders.

I marched toward my office and yanked open the double doors. The faint scent of fresh paint mixed with the vase of peonies hit me as soon as I walked in. A young woman turned, and like everyone else here, she was stunning. Young. *Too young.*

"Mr. Goldsmith, hello, I'm Vivienne. I'm your executive assistant." Curly brown hair and hazel wide-set eyes greeted me with a friendly smile. She held an iPad clutched to her chest.

"Vivienne, call me Ari."

She swallowed the lump in her throat, then smiled. "So today, Mr. Gold, sorry, Ari…" Her eyes drew up to mine for approval, and I nodded. "Your first appointment, Olivia Willows, is at eight o'clock, followed by the board meeting with Farrah at eleven, and marketing is meeting at one o'clock to discuss the upcoming strategy for the fall line. Mr. Sanella would then like a meeting with you at four o'clock."

Ah, to be back and busy. I fucking loved the sound of that.

"Perfect. Let me know when Ms. Willows arrives."

Setting my bag down, I sat in my leather seat, hoping Olivia would do us both a favor and be a no-show.

"Sir, is that all?"

I turned to find Vivienne staring. "Ari, and yes, that's it." I flashed her my smile, and a blush crept on her cheeks before her gaze fell to the floor.

Geez, man, can you stop flirting just for once, or is it embedded in your DNA?

"That's all."

She turned and disappeared. At least one of us was professional.

I gazed around.

My office was back.

Farrah had it vacant all this time.

And now, with my name on the door, highlighted in a shiny plaque with gold block lettering, I felt like I belonged to something. Drifting like a plastic bag in the breeze, I squandered almost a decade away. But here I was, contributing rather than just sleeping my way through town—although that had its benefits.

I wasn't a hit-and-run kind of guy, even though the paparazzi played me that way. Women knew exactly what they were getting into with me. It wasn't like I was promising them the moon. So when we parted, usually after a few nights of fun, it was completely amicable. And the truth was, I was still friends with a lot of the women I had bedded. If you asked me how many, I wouldn't have a clue. But between me, Barrett, Connor, and Magnus, we'd done our fair share of damage. Connor's girlfriend, Pepper, who just moved in with him, nicknamed us the hunkholes. I fucking loved it. We were good-looking and arrogant as fuck too. Why deny women of our gift? May as well own it.

I rolled across the tiled floor, stopping when I hit the block of art-deco windows that opened to Madison Avenue. People walked on the sidewalk, one after the other like well-oiled machines, all rushing to their destinations. I searched for her among the sea of women and spotted a redhead. I stood, zeroing in as my breath pulled inside my lungs. I hoped with everything inside me that it was her. But reality hit hard, and I released my breath, knowing it wasn't.

She was never ever going to be there. Every day since the accident, I searched for Sophia, knowing in my heart she was gone. In a city of millions, I searched, I hoped, and I prayed. Even the countless women who slept in my bed couldn't replace her. Fuck, I tried. Whether it was the hottest celebrity or supermodel I tried burying myself in, they all left the same void. So fucking around to find Sophia turned into fucking to feel whole again. Which worked, for about an hour.

Vivienne stuck her head through the crack of the sliding door, peeling me away from my self-destruction, and I whipped my head around.

"Sir... Ari, sorry. I have Ms. Willows here to see you."

A grin split onto my face. Fuck, I couldn't help it. After our previous sparring sessions, I bet she never thought I'd be her boss. I couldn't wait to torture her even more.

"Send her in." I moved my chair back behind the desk and sat down. Keeping my gaze on my laptop, I didn't bother to look up when the click of her heels against the concrete floor echoed.

The door slid closed behind her, and I typed busily on my laptop, intentionally wanting to annoy her. She shuffled on the spot, and I rolled my lips in on themselves, halting the grin that threatened to spill onto my face.

"Hello, Ari," she clucked, in her commanding voice that scratched like nails down a chalkboard. Fuck, give me the seductive drunk Olivia over this pain in my ass.

I waited a moment, then glanced up at her from my screen. Corporate Olivia wasn't something I was used to, given I'd only seen her when our mutual friends got together. Wearing a high-neck pebble cream blouse and a black skirt that fell to below the knee was domineering and oddly sexy, even though she was more covered than a nun at Sunday service.

"You're late," I replied. "And you can call me Aristotle at work."

"And you can..." she snapped back but quickly stopped herself. Biting her cheek instead, she took a seat and a deep breath, settling herself in for an all-out war. "Yes, I'll make sure the two minutes I'm late won't happen again." Caked in sarcasm, her words dripped like candle wax from her plump lips.

"You'd better."

Her lips pressed into a thin line as she gripped the armrests. She was so unusual-looking. Hair blonde and short, neat and low maintenance, I wondered if that's why she cut it that way—bangs on one side, down to her thick eyebrows and large almond-shaped eyes.

Her eyes narrowed like she was preparing for battle. Bright

but alert and vicious at the same time, her irises were black, surrounded by the deepest blue. Natural makeup, except for her full lips, which were scarlet red and definitely natural too. I hovered over them a moment too long, remembering her taste of berries, then the sound of Cruella clearing her throat smacked me out of my delusion.

As if I'd go there again.

"Well, I'm here now. Should we begin?"

"Farrah Goldsmith entrusted you and your company to redesign her flagship store. Hell, I could think of at least twenty top design firms in New York to do it, so whatever you said to her at the fashion show, you got in her ear, and she chose your company. A company that doesn't have one job to its name."

"Your grandmother is a very intelligent woman, perhaps she studied me and my tenure at Barrett's construction company."

"I doubt it. I told you at dinner, and I'll tell you again. Your work is plain."

Her face bloomed with anger. "You can't talk to me like that, Ari…"

I raised my eyebrows. "It's Aristotle, and if I'm going to repeat myself around here, we won't get anything done… and we have clear deadlines."

"Aristotle!" She hissed through a clenched jaw.

"Good girl, you're catching on."

Her nostrils flared on her delicate nose, and I smirked inwardly.

"I have already sent the briefs to your email. Familiarize yourself with it and meet me downstairs in thirty minutes when we go to the flagship store."

"Together?" Her brows raised in a question. Did she really think I'd leave her all alone to work on the refit rather than ride her coattails?

"Together," I cautioned, staring her down like we were

opponents in a boxing ring. She was wrong if she thought I wouldn't be riding her ass. So very wrong.

"Can't wait." She deadpanned.

"Me too, Ms. Willows. You know where the door is. Don't let it hit you on the way out."

Without waiting for her reply, I reverted my attention to my laptop. She stood, and the huff she released as she yanked her briefcase off the floor caused me to look up. Tattered and worn, could she not afford a new one? She stomped the floor with her chunky patent heels, and her curves sashayed out the door with each step.

Ms. Willows, I will ride that ass the entire time you're here… and something tells me I'm going to enjoy it.

3

OLIVIA

You know where the door is. Don't let it hit you on the way out.
Asshole.

I was a grown woman, for fuck's sake. I didn't need to put up with this. I'd left a perfectly great job with a loyal boss and job security for this? How were Barrett and Ari even friends? They were so different.

Barrett was firm but fair as my old boss, but Ari, Ari wasn't fair. Ari was a silver-spoon baby and playboy whose movie-star appearance might fool the women he beds, but they didn't fool me. Self-righteous and a pompous jerk, he was the one who didn't deserve to be here. Yet he had the audacity to call my work plain. *Twice!*

Ari was so far up himself that he was the definition of overrated.

I trudged behind his assistant, Vivienne. Every step became heavier as anger sparked in my veins. At one point, my steps pounded the tiled floor, and the heel of my Mary Jane shoe wobbled. Dammit, I would not lose a perfectly good shoe over the man.

She called the elevator, and I stepped in as soon as the

doors opened. I went straight toward the back, resting against the cold metal rail where I white-knuckled my briefcase, my fingers stretching so far they burned with the lead grip.

When the doors opened to one floor below, I was tempted to remain in the elevator, hit the ground button, walk out of the building, and never look back. But I couldn't do it. I wouldn't pass up such an opportunity, and more importantly, I wouldn't let Ari win.

Walking out onto oak herringbone, I immediately noticed this floor was very different than the executive level we had just come from. Open-planned desks filled the floor with a handful of offices against the wall. Comfy seating dotted empty spaces among potted palms and ferns. The walls were stamped with oversized photographs of iconic dresses the Farrah Goldsmith House had curated over the last sixty-four years.

I'd done the math. Farrah was only nineteen when she started the label. And she'd done it all by herself. Cue Celine Dion. The woman was a testament to hard work and getting shit done.

"Here is your office, Ms. Willows." Vivienne stopped by a large corner office, having me do the same.

"Really?" I stepped inside. A white desk filled the space, and black steel art deco windows framed both sides, letting in sunlight from all angles and making it light and bright. It was stunning and not in the least what I was expecting.

"Are you sure?" I asked, my previous anger suddenly losing a little steam.

She gazed at me, confused. "Of course."

Immediately, I walked inside and placed my bag on the desk.

"Thank you, Vivienne," I replied.

"Of course. Ms. Willows, I hope you don't mind me asking, but is everything okay?"

I snapped my head up. The last thing I would ever be was

unprofessional at the workplace. "Everything is fine," I replied in an even tone as a forced smile peeled into my cheeks.

"Oh… okay. I'll leave you to settle in."

"Yes, please."

I walked over to the view through the arched windows. Manhattan buzzed below, and unlike modern skyscrapers that blocked out the noise with soundproof glass, the beep of taxi horns and sirens sounded, but that just added to the charm. Street vendors filled the mouths of hungry workers, and lines of people stretched around the corner, waiting for the latest breakfast bar to hit Madison Avenue, *Beurre Moi*—in English, Butter Me Up.

I made a mental note to try it since it was so close. Dario, my roommate, who was in the know of all things culinary because of his sommelier job, implored me to try it. Something about a jam donut inside a croissant.

If I wanted an escape from Ari, that would be the place to go. The man wouldn't ingest that many calories with his rock-hard body, and I sure as hell knew that no one from FGC would be caught dead there. Having a thousand calories for breakfast? Pigs would fly before a model graced *Beurre Moi*. But me? I was French, well—third generation on my mom's side—so it would be a sin not to try the croissant, jammy-ball thingy.

I quickly unpacked my things, knowing I wouldn't have the time to sort, label, and unpack them properly how I liked them, so I just set them down on the desk. I'd get to it later. It pained me to do so because 'order' was my middle name, but there was no way I would be late twice. I imagined Ari above me, laughing at our interlude, and the heat scaled my back, making its way around to the front of my neck, replacing the bliss I felt a moment ago.

I wanted to escape and fold into myself. Instead, I checked my watch. Twenty minutes until I was face-to-face with Captain Fuck Stick downstairs.

Once I had familiarized myself with the brief, I had only a few minutes left. I stood and slipped my phone out of my briefcase. Lourdes' name flashed up with a message on the screen.

Lourde: *Liv, How's it going over at FGC?*

"Ha." Strained laughter escaped my lips and bounced around the empty office.

How exactly was she friends with douchebag Ari? I decided to keep my drunken kiss with Ari to myself. Afterall, no one saw us at Lourde's apartment, so there was no point rehashing that mistake.

I quickly typed out a reply.

Olivia: *Ari, or Aristotle as he has requested I call him, is a bigger dickhead than I thought.*

Three bubbles immediately flashed up on the screen. I picked up my briefcase and headed to the elevator, making sure I wasn't late. Knowing Ari, he would be watching the second hand on his overpriced Patek Philippe watch just to spite me.

My phone vibrated.

Lourde: *Aristotle? He didn't ask you to call him that? Really? Call me tonight x.*

Oh, yes, he did. If only Lourde were here. Perhaps she could be the mediator we so desperately needed rather than training up the new *me* over at Barrett's company and planning her wedding.

I practically begged her to swap. I was more than happy to help Barrett, but Farrah specifically wanted me, and Lourde wanted to stay with Barrett. Fair enough, the guy was her fiancé. Even so, that left me in my current Captain Fuck Stick predicament.

I tucked my phone into my briefcase, then, with a flat palm, slammed the call button on the elevator.

Just as I released my firm slap, the doors opened, and Ari appeared, a smug grin on his perfect face. He was enjoying this way too much.

"I see you're not late this time, Ms. Willows."

Ugh. Go get hit by a bus.

"It appears not," I replied, running my hand down my bangs in frustration. When I looked back at Ari, he was staring at me intently.

Maybe I should try a different tactic. Coach to his ego, kill him with kindness, that kind of thing. *That always works with arrogant jerks, doesn't it? And why was it hot all of a sudden?*

I stepped into the elevator and smiled. "The office is lovely. Thank you," I churned out through a clenched jaw.

"Pleasure."

His arm brushed past my waist as he hit the elevator button, and I jerked back instantly in response. Forgetting he was behind me, I stepped back and hit his chest. Firm like granite, his hands cradled my forearms, his fingers pressing around my arms. He hadn't budged from the weight of my body.

Ari smelled of the ocean and fresh laundry behind a subtle musky aftershave. *Damn.* I sucked in a deep breath, and his hands lingered. Coupled with his scent and muscles, it awoke my dormant libido almost instantly.

Shit, how long had it been?

He lowered his face, and I tilted my head, feeling his breath on my cheek. "Ms. Willows, if you want me, just say so." His voice was gravelly low, and his bravado shook me out of my stance.

I lurched forward but not before an errant shiver went

down my spine, and he immediately removed his hands. Then I turned around squarely, bristling with newfound anger but acutely aware of his lingering touch. "News flash, Aristotle, not every woman wants you."

He laughed, his molten-mocha gaze firmly fixed on mine as the elevator descended. Between us, the air took on a different feel. Sticky and hot, it clogged the air in my lungs.

"They might not know it, but they do." His voice was calm and confident, and it pissed me off. But I wasn't sure if I was upset with his cockiness or my body's reaction to it.

I thrust my hand on my hip, and his eyes dragged down my body. "God complex, seriously?"

"I take what I want, Ms. Willows." He flicked his eyes back up to mine and held them there. "And if I wanted you, I could... easily. I think we both know that."

I whipped my head around, giving him my back. My blood boiled as heat scaled my shoulders and neck. *The gall.* "I was drunk, so were you, Ari. We will not speak of that ever..." But before I could finish muttering my sentence, the doors sprang open to an awaiting Farrah and her assistant.

She stared directly at me and raised a perfectly plucked brow. I straightened, the scowl on my face immediately replaced with a warm smile. "Ms. Goldsmith, good morning."

I slipped out to shake her hand. It was soft, and I remembered grabbing her hand right before she nearly busted a hip tripping over cables at the fashion show. "Call me Farrah, please."

Heavy footsteps echoed behind me. Ari bent down and kissed his grandmother on both cheeks, and I watched his body language shift from cocky asshole to caring grandson. "Aristotle, Olivia, good morning."

"We were just on our way to the store."

"Excellent, I can't wait to see your concepts, Olivia, and I hope my grandson here hasn't been too hard on you."

"Not at all, Farrah," I said tight-lipped, then smiled widely at the old lady. Her weathered brown eyes met mine, and a flash of something was behind them. You could tell this woman had worked every waking hour to get where she was today. Immediately, I was drawn to her dedication and tenacity.

A smile fell from her face. "Ah-ha. That's why I hired you, Olivia. You have the same fire in your eyes like I did all those years ago."

"Thank you, ma'am," I replied. *Well, at least someone appreciates me.*

"Let's go. We don't want to be late again, do we?" Ari glared, annoyance flaring behind his molten eyes.

"Let's meet later this week, Olivia. I'll ask my assistant here to schedule it in."

"Looking forward to it, Farrah."

Turning to find Ari leaps ahead and exiting through the rotating doors that lead out to the street, I hurried behind him with a slight spring in my step.

At least Farrah was a peach. I was determined to prove my worth to her, not Ari. From what I'd heard, he only recently rejoined the couture label that his grandmother owned. Stepping away for nearly a decade, he'd traveled the world and spent his time bedding supermodels. The idea of someone living life that way annoyed me.

What different lives we led. I bet he's never had to wonder where the next meal was coming from. I shook my head as I stepped onto the busy sidewalk. The noise of blaring horns and swirling wind catapulted me into the present moment.

He set a brisk pace. Since there were no contingencies for second place with Ari, I kept up. For the brief minute walk, he spent the time on his phone, and I was grateful for the solace. Finally, free from his whip-smart mouth, I took the time to compose myself after this morning's interrogation.

As we approached, he slowed down and clicked off his

phone, sliding it into his navy suit pocket. The store had construction signs plastered all over it, with white timbers and signage that looked outdated and ratty. Certainly not in keeping with the brand's luxurious label. I made a mental note to change that.

He stopped in front of the door, and I gazed up. Two stories, it held a premier spot on the avenue, prime real estate wedged between Alexander McQueen and Hermes.

"Watch where you step. Or don't." He shrugged, then tossed me a smile, his row of perfectly straight chalk-white teeth taunting me. I narrowed my eyes and gripped my briefcase tighter.

He opened the door. Then as I thought he was going to hold it open for me, he let it go. The big heavy door hit my shoulder, throwing me off balance. Luckily, the doorframe stopped me from falling flat on my face, which he would have liked, no doubt, the sadistic asshole.

"That's one," I warned as I walked inside and literally brushed myself off, sending dust confetti everywhere.

For a split second, I was sure he looked concerned but was sorely mistaken when a grin materialized on his face. "Don't play against me, Ms. Willows… because you will lose."

"You're the one setting the stage for an all-out battle. And you should know by now, I don't bow down… to anyone." I straightened, taking a step closer toward him. "Your grandmother wants me, so that makes me indispensable in her eyes. I couldn't care less what you think, Ari."

There was a challenge behind his mocha-colored eyes, and it held mine. It also set my skin alight with, what was that, rage?

"You're on, Ms. Willows, may the best man win."

"Wo-man, win," I corrected him.

He smiled, and the sun caught his eyes as he held my gaze. The air grew static and thick, and I wondered why things had suddenly gone there again and what the hell I was getting myself into.

"Ari, so good to see you, my friend. It's been too long." A flat-footed man in white overalls and a gray hat descended the staircase. I watched Ari's posture change from stiff and ramrod straight to relaxed. He hurried toward the man. "Pedro. I should have guessed Grandmama had you here on the job." He hugged the older man, not caring if his tailored suit was now dusty.

Ari towered over the man. Actually, Ari towered over everyone. His broad shoulders and thick forearms nearly swallowed the man whole.

"How was your break from the company?" Pedro asked with a geniality in his tone.

Would you really call ten years a break?

"Fine."

"I hope it was everything you needed, son." The old man and Ari exchanged a look that I certainly wasn't privy to.

What was that about?

Ari turned to me, his eyes dark as they held mine. I shifted my weight from one foot then the other, feeling like a third wheel.

"And this lovely woman must be Olivia." As though sensing my discomfort, Pedro walked toward me. Fine salt and pepper hair spilled from underneath his cap, and a red button nose and cheerful face greeted me. He exuded warmth like Santa and my old man. I immediately liked him. He reminded me of my father, who I should really pay a visit since he and Mom had been complaining I hadn't seen them in so long.

"Nice to meet you, Pedro." I held out my hand for him to shake, but he bypassed it and leaned it to kiss me on one cheek, then the other.

I smiled nervously, not used to such informality in the workplace.

I felt Ari's gaze upon me, but I kept my attention on the cheerful old man in front of me.

"Let me show you around," he offered, tugging on his coveralls.

"Pedro is the site manager for a lot of our redevelopments. He works closely with our contractors and has been with the company for forty years."

"Well, I look forward to hitting the ground running with you, Pedro."

Putting down my briefcase in a space where I thought there was the least amount of dust, I pulled out my notebook and pen while sliding my phone into my suit pocket.

Ari raised an eyebrow, curiously assessing me. "What's that for?"

"Phone for photos, notepad for notes... obviously." The last part I said under my breath so Pedro, a few steps ahead, couldn't hear. Professionalism was my second middle name.

"If you were vigilant, you would know the brief included measurements and photos."

Clutching my phone, notepad, and pencil, I tsked. "I don't like to rely on other people's work."

"And by other people, you mean the professionals?" He scoffed.

"They have got things wrong."

He folded his arms and watched me gather the rest of my things, and by things, I meant my trio of colored pens and sticky notes. Yes, call me what you want—anal, methodical—I had heard them all, but I always got the job done my way. I ignored his patronizing and the way his jacket curved around his biceps.

"We have people to measure up, Ms. Willows."

"Your grandmother paid me to do a job, and this is the job that I do to the best of my ability. I don't take any shortcuts."

Pedro turned around from halfway up the staircase, his

warm eyes like saucers, a smile on his mouth. "Brains and beauty." Pedro laughed, and I shrunk back into myself. I hadn't intended on him hearing our petty chat, but he had. Let's just hope it didn't leave these walls.

Ari walked ahead of me. "If you think that ol' man, you are more senile than I thought."

A horsey laugh left Pedro's mouth as he walked up the remaining stairs. I held my head high, not wanting Ari to see how annoyed I was inside.

My heels clicked against the bare stairs stripped back, ready for coverings. When I reached the last step, I walked into the upstairs area. It was a large room, but smaller than downstairs, and my mind went into overdrive. Immediately, I went to work with ideas. Scribbling on the pad in my hand, I visualized lots of oak, tan leathers, and sophisticated accents of gold and purples throughout. The place was dark, so oak would suit better than mahogany or walnut, but ideas were floating in and out so quickly I couldn't keep up with my scribbling.

I'd been at it a while when I overheard Pedro ask Ari about his love life. In particular, one, Juliette Mayer. You lived under a rock if you hadn't heard of Supermodel and It Girl, Juliette Mayer. Think Gigi Hadid or Gisele Bundchen. And if TMZ had it right, which, let's be honest, they rarely did, she'd dumped Ari and was now going out with celebrity chef, Anders Wilmer.

"Jealous?" Pedro asked Ari.

Intently, I glanced up from my notes, curious about Ari's reaction.

"Not at all. We had our fun." He deadpanned, completely detached from any feeling whatsoever.

A snorty sound left my nose, and shit, that wasn't meant to happen. I stared at them both in alarm. *Could I be any more unprofessional?*

Immediately, both men turned and looked in my direction.

I looked from Pedro to Ari. Ari rubbed the base of the stubble on his chin, his mocha eyes and confidence making me want to crawl back into a hole.

A curiosity and question held behind his eyes. "Did you want to add something, Ms. Willows?"

"No, nothing," I quickly responded, wanting to change the entire subject before I drowned in my humiliation and unprofessionalism. "So I've seen enough up here. I'm going downstairs to review my notes."

"Good, because I have an eleven o'clock meeting, and time is important to me, Ms. Willows."

And women aren't? I wanted to add but refrained, only just.

"Of course." *Asshole.*

I slid my pencil back into the pencil holder of my folder and held the folder to my blouse as I descended the spiral staircase. Being unprofessional wasn't me. But it was not even lunchtime, and Ari had made me stoop to his level.

Well, if he wanted me to do my job, I was not backing down. This could be an all-out war of the wills, and I would not lose, not when everything I'd worked so hard for was on the line.

4

ARI

Damn, it was good to be back, especially since I was walking into my four o'clock now and squaring off with William, or Sanella as we all called him. Farrah's Vice President and the man who had been steering the FGC ship since I up and left years ago.

On the executive level, he'd steered clear of me today and I, him.

He worked for me all those years ago, and deep down, part of me always knew he resented working for the owner's grandson, who was half his age. He was always friendly, though, especially when Grandmama made me meet her in her office before going to our regular lunches over the years.

Personally, I thought she did that to remind me of what I was missing out on, and maybe it worked. Grinding me down with the familiar environment long enough, she knew I'd come back, eventually. And I guess I did. But some things changed and some things didn't ever. I might be back, but my guilt remained. That was something that could never be erased.

Sanella's assistant greeted me with a friendly smile. "Mr.

Goldsmith, I'm Rebecca. Come on in. Please, go ahead. He is expecting you."

"Thanks, Becca." I tossed her my smile.

"Sir." Her cheeks warmed the color red. Then her eyes drifted down to the screen in front of her.

God, was I seriously flirting? I'm addicted. I did it without realizing it.

I pushed the door open, and Sanella peered up from his paperwork. Immediately, he stood and walked around to greet me.

"Ari, so nice to see you again and in this capacity."

My extended hand did nothing as the man hugged the shit out of me in some old man embrace I couldn't wait to get out of. One old man was enough, and even he wasn't this forthcoming.

I quickly removed myself from his embrace and hauled my ass over to the leather armchair, resting my forearms on the metal arm rests.

"It's great to be back," I offered, fully aware that his over-the-top greeting was his way to butter me up. A hidden warning, perhaps. A hug that meant something like, hey, you're her grandson, and you are back, but back the fuck up, I've been here way longer.

He collapsed into his chair, and it pulled away from the desk. He had the other corner office. Large and expansive views similar to mine were captivating even from the sixth floor.

"So what can I do for you, Sanella?"

"Now, now, we don't want to talk shop just yet. I thought I'd welcome you back and let you know what's been happening here in the last decade or so… we certainly aren't the same business we were when you left us."

Yeah? No shit.

When I left, you were working under me. My leaving paved the way to where you are today. Don't fucking forget it.

The back and forth that continued for the next half hour reminded me of the same battle I had with Olivia. Except at least she was blonde, fit, and extremely and yet, unusually pretty. She'd pull more than craned necks if it weren't for that foul mouth and fiery personality.

That tussle had me more intrigued than I thought it would. I buzzed from within, knowing I could get under her skin and, oh, that buttery skin. When she fell back on me this morning, my body responded. She smelled of sweet roses and rosemary, and immediately it took me back to when my lips crashed down on hers.

"I hear you have a great designer leading the redesign of the store." His comment whacked me out of the weird Olivia world I was in.

"Yes, that's right."

Sanella was certainly not privy to our tit and tat, that special battle was purely between Olivia and me, and although I called her work plain, it was only to piss her off more, like she had me. Call me sadistic, but I got off seeing her livid as fuck. Because that's exactly what she did to me when she challenged everything I said and called me a womanizer.

"Well, I'd like to meet her."

I'm sure you would, you dirty old man. "Of course."

He stared at me as though waiting for something, his thick brows unruly and unkempt, arching at me with a question not asked.

"What, now?" I asked, thinking why the sudden need to meet Olivia.

"Now is better than any other time," he said, closing the folder on his desk and standing.

Well, why not? It had only been a few hours since I'd seen her this morning. I was going to swing by and see her before I left anyway.

"Right. Follow me then."

The man struggled to keep pace. He must have been in his fifties now, but that wasn't old. He was overweight and a chain smoker. If Farrah wasn't riddled with arthritis, I'm sure even in her eighties, she would have whooped his ass in a sprint down these hallways.

As I walked toward the elevators, sounds left his mouth as he huffed with each overweight step he took. Lazy prick, if he hit the gym with me, he wouldn't get back up for weeks.

We rode the elevator one floor down, and as the doors opened, employees turned, then immediately went back to work. Sanella was quite a taskmaster with the staff, and from the response, I could see it was definitely the truth. I wondered if Grandmama was aware of his managerial style. She must be. Otherwise, she wouldn't keep him on all these years.

Just let it go, Ari. It's day one.

"Word is, your little designer has a tight ass and is very flexible."

I held my hand out, forcing him to stop before we approached her office. Anger bloomed in my legs, making its way to a lump in my throat. Olivia got under my skin, but that didn't give him free rein to talk about her like a piece of ass.

"What are you doing?" he bristled, brushing my hand away from his pot belly. "It's true. Jeffrey saw her dating profile on Matchmaker.com. Whoa, is she flexible!"

An uncomfortable feeling settled in the pit of my stomach. Sanella waved his hand in the air and continued walking.

"Sanella, you are an employee of this company, just like Olivia. I expect employees to be respectful of each other."

"Please, this coming from Manhattan's playboy?" He laughed a haughty laugh which turned into a chesty cough.

The man was disgusting.

Before I could warn him again, he opened her office door,

without knocking and slid in there like the slippery snake he was.

Sanella had a reputation among the models—think Harvey Weinstein—and even though Olivia was a thorn in my side, I had a duty to protect her from him.

"You must be the beautiful Olivia. I've heard a lot of interesting things about you."

Olivia, hard at work, shook out of her concentration. Her gaze lifted abruptly to Sanella, then to me, finally resting back on Sanella as she stood to greet him.

"Hello, and you must be Mr. Sanella." Her smile was friendly, but the ice behind her eyes told a different story. She didn't like his tone, and neither did I.

Luckily, she hadn't heard what he said before.

"That's me."

"What are you working on there?" He moved up to her table, sitting on the corner, his stomach spilling onto his leg. *Geez, man, haven't you heard of the gym?*

She hovered nearby, creating more space between them. "Just a few sketches for the new store."

I came closer, brushing past her, and regarded her sketches. They were impressive, a free-hand sketch, when we had computers to do all that and in that small amount of time. She'd mapped out the entire store—both levels. Beside her were more pages of sketches. *She had a Plan B?* She had designed more than one mockup in a few hours.

Impressive. Not that I'd tell her that.

"So where are you from, gorgeous?" Sanella's eyes cast down to the front of her dress, overtly and painfully obvious. It made the contents of my breakfast lurch into my throat.

"If you don't mind, I prefer Olivia, sir. And I'm from Brooklyn."

Well, damn.

Sanella lifted his eyes to her face. "I don't mind at all," he said in a creepy voice and split into a cheesy grin. I wanted to reach across the table and wipe it off with a razor blade.

Olivia's nostrils flared, and when she turned, her eyes slammed into mine. The question behind her eyes went something like, "Why the fuck did you bring him?"

Seeing a woman in discomfort wasn't my thing, so I stepped in.

"Sanella, didn't you say you had a five o'clock in manufacturing? You probably don't want to keep them waiting?"

Olivia widened her eyes, and she tipped her head to the side. *Yes, believe it, Olivia, but this was more for me than you.*

He turned and faced me, a gruff scowl on his face. "Dammit. To be continued, *Olivia*," he boomed, pronouncing her name with a louder tone for effect.

"Of course." Her lips drew into a thin line, and this time, she wasn't meeting his gaze with a smile.

Sanella turned to face me. "Ari, see you later in the week to talk shop. Becca will set it up."

As he disappeared, I watched her watch him walk away. Her body held rigid and straight, the sunlight turning the circles of her irises into light blue Tahitian waterfalls framed by dark, long eyelashes. I shook myself out of whatever the hell that was, especially since now that same pointed stare was aimed directly at me.

"Thanks for that," she said, almost begrudgingly.

Well, she didn't need to thank me.

"I didn't do it for you, princess. I know you can handle yourself."

She stared up at me, her expression unreadable.

"Right." She sat back down, flicking through her sketches. It was obvious she wanted me to leave. But I didn't move. I just stood in front of her, my six-foot-four height casting a shadow from the lights above onto her desk.

And her desk. How was it so... perfect? I looked around,

and my eyebrows drew further north, more in horror than surprise. Neat was an understatement. She was goddamn anal. A stapler here, pencils lined up in spectrum rainbow order there, to the right were design books. *No, they weren't, were they?* "Have you alphabetized the books?" I asked, leaning over her desk and tapping on the neat stack of books.

She turned to her stack of books, then back at me. "So what if I have?" She breathed out, and her warmth hit my cheek.

I grinned in response. Ah, she was back. "You are stranger than I thought, Ms. Willows."

"You're just as I thought you were, Aristotle."

I grinned, unmoving. My gaze hovered over hers, and she held it like a game of chess. In my peripheral vision, I saw her chest rise and fall quickly, her irises blackening from the increased pulse.

My gaze slipped from her eyes down to her lips. Slightly parted and slick with red gloss, I let my mind wander. My breathing quickened as the air grew thick like a sauna. Were they parted before, or did she want me to kiss her?

No, the woman was ice.

As soon as I realized what I was doing, I snapped out of it.

"I hope you have a Plan C, Ms. Willows, 'cause I think you'll need it."

I pushed off her desk, my legs oddly heavy. Her eyes grew like saucers atop her thin nose that flared with anger.

For effect, I widened my eyes.

"Of course I do," she slammed back in a stern voice.

"Good. I expect it on my desk in the morning."

I walked out of her office, straight to the elevators, and down to the lobby, where I burst out onto the sidewalk for some air. My dick knocked against my trouser seams.

What the fuck was that?

And why did I imagine her laying spread-eagled on my solid oak desk?

5

OLIVIA

I'd tried to ignore him as much as possible since my harrowing Monday on the job and considering we'd come face to face literally in an awkward show of wills. When his face was so close to mine, I could have reached out and strangled him. But that would have messed up his tailored suit. Up close, he was even prettier—mocha-colored eyes, tanned golden smooth skin, and thick full lips shielding a row of perfectly straight teeth. Could the man be more perfectly carved? Seriously, it was revolting.

But when his gaze drifted to my lips, I heard my heart pounding in my chest so loudly it knocked the wind from my sails. Confusion rained down on me like a tsunami warning, but that's when I knew exactly what he was doing. Ari, the playboy of Manhattan, knew how to charm women, and if he wasn't torturing me with unspeakable deadlines, he would do what was in his DNA. It was his second nature, so I thought nothing of it until immediately after he asked me to sketch a third set of plans when it was the end of the day and have it ready for him the following morning. No. I had no time to think about his thick lips or the way my body pulled toward his. I wanted to slap him when he got under my skin. Instead, I burned the midnight oil getting the plans drawn up so they were on his desk before he came in on Tuesday morning. And I made sure they were there before he got in because I wouldn't give Ari the satisfaction of them not being there. No, sir.

Thursday came around like a whirlwind, and I'd been so busy planning the flagship store I had barely eaten. I looked up at the fluorescent lighting, and my head felt light and fuzzy.

It was four o'clock, and I had only a glass of water in me and a pack of salt and vinegar potato chips. Not great for someone with low blood sugar. I focused on the plant outside my office, anything to straighten my focus. Vibrant forest green and yellow heart-shaped leaves cascaded down an Aztec patterned pot. Nature was a marvel. Why had I only just noticed it after being here nearly a week?

Because you work yourself to the bone, girl.

I shook away the thought and leaped up from my chair, which wasn't a great idea as my balance wavered. I steadied myself on the desk with both hands and took a deep breath.

There is a reason you're a workaholic. Look where you are now.

I nodded and gingerly headed out the door and made my way toward the elevators. But instead of going down to the busy Manhattan sidewalk and hitting up the local café, I thought I'd try out the in-house kitchen. Truthfully, I needed food immediately, and I wasn't sure if I would make it to the café, then have to wait for my order to arrive.

Vivienne, Ari's assistant, had mentioned the executive kitchen on the top floor—the executive floor on level six. That would have to do. I pressed the button, and the doors closed.

When they opened, I walked out, careful not to bump into the grinch that was my boss. I avoided his line of sight as much as possible, banking left rather than right near the row of offices—a slightly longer way but necessary.

I pulled the door open and closed it behind me. All sorts of smells invaded my senses and my stomach rumbled in response. Pre-made salads, sashimi, sandwiches, and acai yogurt bowls filled the open shelves of the refrigerated display. My mouth watered.

Warmers had cooked sliced meats, curries, soups, and some kind of pre-made omelet thing.

All healthy, all expected. No burgers and fries here.

Famished, I grabbed a bowl of chicken curry and located a steamer full of rice. Happily, I scooped a healthy ladle of wild rice—of course—into the small bowl nearby and placed both on the small table at the far end of the kitchen. Aromas of lemongrass and jasmine surrounded my nostrils as I held up the curry to my mouth and shoveled it in. One scoop after another, the bowl emptied. The food was delicious, and I'd eaten the entire thing in under five minutes, and yet, I was still hungry.

My gaze lifted to the other refrigerator for a closer inspection, and my eyes widened. *How did I miss that?*

At the bottom of the display was a row of chocolate bars. I picked one up, ninety percent cocoa. Okay, so healthy chocolate bars. Peeling off the foil wrapper, I took a large bite, taking the entire first two rows in my mouth. I let the velvety chocolate melt on my tongue for a few seconds, savoring the taste before swallowing it.

Not like my normal cookies and creme Hershey's bar, this was slightly bitter and very rich in flavor. Not bad, actually.

The door swung open, nearly hitting me. To avoid getting slammed into, I jerked to the side, dropping my chocolate bar. It landed in front of extra-large pointy tan shoes. Shoes that belonged to *him*. Hmm, if big feet were anything to go by, maybe those rumors were true.

Ari stopped and picked up my chocolate bar, the door closing behind him.

"Chocolate, Ms. Willows?" He held up the bar, the wrapper hanging off it as he smirked that cheeky-as-fuck smile on his golden face.

"Ten points for you, Aristotle."

He narrowed his eyes at me, then turned toward the trash.

"What are you doing?" I half-yelled, reaching for his arm before he threw it away. I shuffled so I was in front of him and the trash, trying to block him from throwing away a good chocolate bar.

He stared down at me, his velvet eyes piercing into my ribcage and squeezing my breath into my throat.

"I'm throwing away the chocolate."

"Why?" I asked, my hand atop his stone biceps.

He looked at me like I had a feather growing out of my ears.

"Because it hit the floor, Ms. Willows."

"Only for a second. I'll have it back, please." I reached for the wrapper, but with ease, he swatted me away.

"Not going to happen, sweetheart."

I heard the chocolate hit the trash can, and anger bloomed inside my chest. I huffed out a loud sigh and turned my back to him. How many times had I wondered as a child when or if our next meal would come? Or would Mom and Dad watch me eat, happily forgoing a meal themselves so I wouldn't starve? Saying they already ate when I knew for a fact they hadn't.

No, Ari had never experienced hunger. He'd never experienced hardship. His only difficulty was probably flying coach instead of first class.

"Here, have another one." His condescending tone echoed around the executive kitchen, smacking me between the feels.

I turned around with a tornado force, falling into his granite chest.

His hand sank into my waist, his thumb against the silk of my blouse pressed into my stomach, striking a match with the connection. "This is becoming a habit, Ms. Willows." His voice sounded like gravel and sin.

Startled, I blinked a few times, then tilted my head up from his broad chest. The steady draw of his dreamy brown eyes emptied every single thought from my mind.

No. No. No.

Thoughts came back quickly, and I pushed away the short-circuit brain fart I just had. I was angry. He wouldn't placate me with chocolate eyes and perfectly swept dark brown hair.

"There was nothing wrong with that chocolate bar. You've just been wasteful." I arched my back, creating some well-needed space between us, but his hand remained burning on my skin.

"If I'd known it meant that much to you, Ms. Willows, I would have happily given it back."

I blinked. Did I hear him correctly? Why was he being so kind?

"Then I could watch you eat it off the floor it shares with the rodents."

"Ugh!" I palmed both hands on his chest, pushing out of his grasp. "You've got no idea." I slammed my bowl and cutlery into the dishwasher, angry with myself for letting his touch and scent of his aftershave divert my attention. "I bet you have no idea of the price of milk," I muttered under my breath.

"Careful, Ms. Willows." His voice was bitter, causing me to turn.

His eyes darkened, and his body stiffened. Good, I'd crawled under his skin now like he had inched his way into mine.

"Do you then?"

He stepped closer, and automatically I reached behind me, finding the counter to steady myself. His navy suit brushed up against my blouse and skirt. He was so close. *Did he do this with all his staff?*

Was he angry or was he... his gaze hovered, drifting to my lips. I stopped breathing. His hand circled my chin, tilting it up to his face. His eyes dragged up to mine, and there was an unmistakable fire behind them. I wanted more. I leaned in closer, my body betraying me.

"I suggest you wipe the remnants of that curry off those full lips... or I will."

What? I blinked, unsure if I heard him correctly, then held my hand to my mouth.

Oh, God. I felt something that had no place being there on my mouth. Quickly, I located a napkin on the counter and took it to my lips, wiping away the morsel of food. When I looked up again, he was gone. The only sign of him ever being here was the half-open door and the irritation and confusion pooling in my stomach.

6

ARI

Returning to my office, I sat in my chair, staring vacantly at the screen. I shouldn't have said that. She made me lose my head. When she was near, all thought went out the window like a groom on his bachelor's night. I wanted to throw her off. Cast her off the scent she was on. I had to. I couldn't tell her the price of a gallon of milk, but so what? Did that make me any less of a man? No. But she made another assumption about me, and that got my back up. So much so, I couldn't let her win that battle even though the thought of my mouth on hers again had my arousal peeking.

She thought she knew me.

She knew nothing about me.

Like society, she prejudged me. Stamping her labels and judgments on me like a Black Friday sale. Rich boy, womanizer, arrogant. But I saw the way she stared back at me. Or the way her body instinctively leaned into mine when I had her close.

Out of all the women I'd ever known, she was the one who crawled under my skin and left me with a nasty rash. But I couldn't get her out of my mind. Like a lingering STD, she hovered around, itching and flaring when she was near. There was no escaping her. I'd tried this week, somewhat on purpose, and because Sanella had thrown me a curveball and asked me to manage something he should be handling. But as much as I didn't want to admit it, Olivia was on top of the redesign of the flagship store, so I knew I could leave her to plan it. The three sketches I made her do in record time were all possible and viable solutions for the store revamp.

She'd come up with unique designs that impressed me, and the truth was, I didn't impress easily.

When my phone pinged, I slid it out of my suit jacket. It was a group chat with the boys.

I clicked on the message and noticed I had missed quite a few, so I scrolled back to play catch up.

Barrett: *Boys, it's my sister's birthday, and I've convinced her to come down to Manhattan for the weekend. Who's up for a party?*

Magnus: *I'm always up for a party.*

Connor: *Yes, Pepper and I are in.*

Magnus: *Eye roll emoji. Of course, you two are.*

Connor: *Haven't got your dick wet, Magnus?*

Magnus: *Did last night… twice. Thank you very much.*

Barrett: *Ari, you in?*

I thumbed out a reply.

Me: *I'm in. Where and when.*

Barrett: *My place. Friday night, 7 p.m. Don't be late. It's a surprise.*

Magnus: *Girls?*

Barrett: *Only a few, Magnus. Ari?*

Connor: *Yeah, Ari, call up your black book.*

I snorted out a laugh, and Vivienne, my assistant, looked up with doe eyes I'd recently come to loathe. *Was I just a pretty face?* Since being back, staff, namely beautiful women, which was everyone in this place, had come up with any excuse to book a meeting with me. At first, it was enjoyable. Now, it was downright annoying.

Peeling me away from my work to have meaningless chats about the fall line and if her hair color looked better in shades of orange or burned honey. Fuck me, but if she continued to stare at me that way, she would be fired. I shot her back a steely glance, then slammed my door behind me.

Walking over to my office chair, I sat down and typed out a reply.

Ari: *Sure, I'll message a few and see if they're up for it.*
Barrett: *Not many, Ari. Evelyn doesn't like crowds.*
Connor: *See if they're up for it? Have you ever known models to turn the golden boy Ari down?*
Ari: *Fuck off, Connor. Now some of us have to work to get through.*
Barrett: *Like me.*
Connor: *And me.*

Three dots appeared on the screen under Magnus' name.

Magnus: *Well fuck then, might go get myself another margarita and sit by the pool while you boys waste a shit-hot fall Thursday in the office.*

I sighed. Magnus ought to get a life. Since he found his wife cheating on him, he'd been wallowing in self-pity and getting day drunk like he was a resident Vegas DJ. Mind you, I'd been there, done that.

But my wallowing and self-pity were still going on. I'd slowed down in the sleeping around but drinking and feeling a shit-ton of guilt, well, that remained like the image of her lifeless body in my arms after the car accident.

Blood dripped from her head smashing the glass. She was already dead by the time I got to her, managing to free myself from the wreckage. The coroner told me she died on impact and didn't suffer. So was that meant to bring me some kind of comfort, some kind of twisted, fucked-up sense of relief?

If anything, it made me angrier, and as the years rolled on and I had drunk myself into guilt-ridden oblivion, I turned into a man that had no semblance of my former self. A shadow of a man, who, at twenty-three, had the world at his feet, a fiancée, and a burgeoning career under the guidance of my grandmama at Farrah Goldsmith Couture.

A faint tap pulled at my attention. "Come in," I yelled at the interruption more forcefully than I should have.

"Aristotle, there you are."

I stood immediately, walking over to where my grandmama stood in the doorframe. She looked frailer than earlier in the week if that were possible. Instantly, I felt guilty for the way I just spoke to her.

"Grandmama, you could have called. I would have come to your office." I quickly looped her hand into mine and assisted her to the seat in my office.

"I am fine to walk on my own, you know," she grumbled.

"Hardly, and you don't have your walking stick, so best to lean on me."

She let out a sigh and reluctantly wrapped her arthritic fingers around my forearm.

"Perhaps if you hadn't insisted on keeping these checkered floors polished to a diamond shine, I could leave the unassisted walking to you."

"Oh, you're on fire today, aren't you." Gingerly she fell to the chair, pushing back a stray black hair that fell out of place as she drew in a settling breath. Waiting until I sat down to speak, I got the sense that something was troubling her.

"I can deal with a broken hip. What I can't deal with is cash bleeding from the business I built from the ground up." Her mouth held in a straight line, her jaw firmly set.

I extended my arms along the desk, wondering what the hell she was talking about. "Bleeding cash?"

"I don't know. The accounting team can't account for it. I need someone I can trust to investigate, and that's you, Aristotle."

I interlaced my fingers, not liking the concern behind her tired eyes.

"What's going on, Grandmama?"

"There is around four million missing from the books. Unaccounted for."

"*What?*" I rounded out in a yell, but Grandmama just let out a sigh. "How is that possible? Did you ask accounting to go back over the years to audit the books?"

"They can't find it."

I jerked in my seat. "Well, that's just not good enough."

She slumped a little lower in her seat, and my heart squeezed at her fragility and helplessness. "No, not nearly."

"Do you think it's an inside job?"

"It has to be."

"Who?"

"I don't like to point fingers without proof." She drummed her manicured nails along the cold steel arms of the chair.

"Drummond, the head of accounting? He must be involved."

"Yes, maybe." She nodded, already two steps ahead, thinking of a list of possible culprits. "Maybe it's bigger than him."

Resolute in putting a plug on the leak, I slammed my fist against the desk. "I'm on it, Grandmama. Don't you worry."

"Thank you, Aristotle."

She propped upright. "Now tell me, how is the beautiful Olivia coming along with the store plans?"

"She's busting my balls like I told you she would."

"Come now. Show me what she's got. I could not meet

with her this week as this new development has occupied all my time."

I pulled out the folder she left on my desk and passed it over to her. "Here."

She looked up at me and took the folder, opening it curiously.

Grandmama stared at the first sketch. With the measurement perfect and intricate, it actually gave the definition of sketch a bad name.

"Oh." She sighed in glee.

"There's more," I offered

She licked her index finger, then flicked behind Plan A to Plan B.

More *oohs* and *aahs* came from her as she meticulously scanned the plans. Then she laughed when she arrived at the final sketch.

"Ari, how long have you had these?"

"She had them on my desk Tuesday morning."

She closed the folder shut and moved to stand.

"Wait," I said as I leaped out of my chair, the force pushing it back.

She swatted me away. "I'm fine." Then she stood tall for a woman in her eighties regardless of the scoliosis curving her spine.

"These are remarkable, Ari."

"I know." I split into a thin smile.

"And you don't seem pleased about it." She tapped me on the arm.

"She's talented, sure, but she is so frustrating, Grandmama."

She chuckled, and I rolled my eyes.

"Perhaps you've met your match then." Again, she batted my hand away as I helped her out the door. I shadowed her instead.

"Perhaps you should stick to designing award-winning gowns."

She made it to the door, and I opened it for her. Then she held her hand up to my cheek, a full extension of her arm to reach up high.

"Be kind to yourself, Aristotle." She held my eyes in a tender warning. "Let me know what you uncover and use whatever resources you need."

I nodded. "I will."

"Vivienne, can you please get Ms. Goldsmith's walking stick from her office and hurry back to give it to her? If she will not let me walk her across the floor, then the stick will."

"Yes, sir." Vivienne leaped up quicker than a groupie heading backstage at a concert and briskly headed toward her office.

Grandmama turned and rolled her eyes at me. "Ugh."

"Don't take another step, Grandmama."

"Did you ever think you were the annoying one, not Olivia," She huffed out in frustration, and I closed the door behind me, a smile forming on my lips.

7

OLIVIA

Don't judge me.

I had five minutes to spare, and I mean, it was right there in my bedside drawer, so I reached for my battery-operated boyfriend and lay on the bed. Opening my legs, I let my mind wander.

Yes, this is what I needed. To unwind. To not think about work and… ooh… damn, that feels so good. Yes. Right. There.

I let out a moan and shut my eyes. I was close. *How was I so close so soon?*

My back arched off the bed as heat scaled up my stomach. Dirty, arrogant mocha-colored eyes stared back at me, and the feeling of his lips on mine tipped me over the edge. I let out a moan as stars floated into view.

Holy fuck.

I just came with Ari on my mind.

* * *

"Well, would you look at you," Lourde exclaimed as I stepped out of the elevator into Barrett's penthouse and pulled me into a hug. I'd been missing my friend and business partner so much this week, I held her close.

"Beautiful and cuddly." She released me, oblivious to the exhausted state I was in.

"Is that new?" she asked, her gaze hovering over my black sweetheart dress that just covered my thighs.

"This old thing? Nope, just added the scarf." I thrust out a hip and pointed to the toffee-colored scarf cinching at my waist and making my little black dress appear brand new.

"Love it. I think working at a fashion house has inspired you," Lourde admired and shook her head animatedly, raking a hand through her brown locks and twisting the ends.

"God, if you thought Barrett's company only hires beautiful women, take a walk through the first few levels of Farrah Couture, and you really won't eat again," I huffed out and pushed down my toes in my heels, wondering why I was getting frustrated by the beauties at Farrah Couture but not Barrett's company.

She let out a laugh. "Model Central, hey?"

"Yeah, the skinny supermodel type too, not the type that grace *Sports Illustrated,* at least they have hips and curves."

"I'll pass, thanks… skip the building and treat myself to a pastry at what's that new place called?"

"*Beurre Moi,*" I said. "And yeah, it's the real deal. That jam-croissant concoction is an orgasm on a plate. I tried it this week. You know, after the week from hell I had, I needed a sugar fix."

"I can't believe I haven't tried it yet, especially…" She let her voice waver before continuing. "Has it really been that bad with Ari?" she asked.

I let out a laugh. "Don't even go there."

"Okay, okay. So tell me about *Beurre Moi…*"

Not only did we bond over our love of decorating, but we were foodies, through and through.

She hooked her arm through mine, and we walked through the foyer and past the kitchen. I'd been here before, once when I worked for Barrett and had to drop something off to him, but the place looked different. Previously, it was modern and minimal, but now, color flooded the living room with fuchsia and royal blue pops of color in the cushions and textiles.

"I think Pepper and Connor will be here soon. Magnus is already here with Ari and his little black book of models."

"Ari's here?" I halted, my thin stiletto heels squeaking against the polished floor.

"Shit. I didn't mention that, did I?" Lourde ran a hand through the ends of her chestnut hair and stared at me with a sketchy look on her porcelain face.

She never once mentioned he would be here, and in the single conversation and the handful of texts exchanged this week, I had blurted out my intolerable working conditions with a hellish boss. I told her I wanted to quit, and she begged me to stay. I left out the connection in the elevator and the kitchen because that was Ari just being an arrogant womanizing jerk, thinking every girl would fall for his mocha-colored hypnotic eyes and ridiculous six-pack of muscles that no doubt hid underneath his tailored suit. And my arousal, well, that was due to the lack of action.

I chewed on the inside of my cheek. "No, you didn't mention that, Lourde!"

"Okay, look, we will deal with that later. Barrett just texted me. He's pulling into the garage with his sister, Evelyn, now." She pulled my hand and dragged me toward the crowd of people hovering on the balcony.

"Everyone, quiet. They're here!" Lourde shrieked like a teacher in front of a classroom, and the loud conversations boiled down to a simmer as Lourde corralled people inside. "Quickly move behind the wall so they can't see us."

I locked eyes with Ari. As the tallest guy here, he wasn't hard to spot. But had he spotted me first?

When everyone else was moving, he stayed put, pressed against the cement wall in his baby blue shirt with the sleeves rolled up and black fitted jeans that clung to his thighs. He was annoyingly handsome if only he weren't a dick.

My body flared with agitation, the week from hell looping in my mind like a worn-out record.

My work was plain.

Don't let the door hit you on the way out.

Ugh. So immature. So juvenile. I was a grown woman, for God's sake. And why was he still staring?

"Come on, come on, be quiet!" Lourde cautioned in a firm whisper. Her comment pulled me away from his stare.

Had he known I was going to be here?

Was he annoyed too?

What had I ever done to him anyway for him to hate me so much?

"Olivia, come quick." Pepper reached for my arm, pulling me across to where Connor and Magnus were already standing and hidden from view.

"Pepper, hey!" I whispered while clamoring and huddling with the rest of the group.

"Ari, what are you doing over there? Come here, quickly." Pepper huffed, annoyance flashing across her face.

I turned, and his eyes were still on me. He walked a few yards where we were all hiding behind a wall, but instead of standing near Magnus and the boys, he stepped right in front of me. "Hello, Olivia," he said in a gravelly voice that was like a shot of adrenaline between my thighs. Then he smiled slightly before turning and giving me his back.

So it was Olivia outside of work, but Ms. Willows at work? I could play along too.

"Ari," I whispered back, twisting my lips into a smile.

He lifted his head slightly and nodded. Perhaps he was

coming to appreciate the sass I threw back at him. I bet his Rolodex of models just caved at his every whim. Either that or I was wearing him down like a nail file, one remark at a time.

Maybe he wasn't all man. Like men I'd dated in the past, they couldn't handle me either. Too sassy. Too career driven. Those were some reasons lousy exes had given me. The truth was, they just couldn't handle me. No one could. Maybe I would be alone anyway.

"Olivia?" Pepper pulled at the hem of my dress.

"Huh?" I realized everyone was now cowering down. Even the playboy man in front of me was crouching, his jeans wrapping tightly around his firm ass.

So? A girl could look. He was eye candy, and I hadn't gotten any in over a year. What's the big deal? I could look and ignore the asshole personality and still admire his handsome features like the next girl. It didn't mean anything. Withstanding his charms was easy when he was Captain Fuck Stick.

With my knees bent, I balanced on the balls of my feet, not easy in stilettos, but I never cowered to a challenge. I wobbled, let out a gasp, then regained my balance.

Hurry up, Barrett and Evelyn! Crashing headfirst into my boss' butt would not be a fitting end to my week.

"You're struggling. Hold on to me," he said, turning round, his voice possessive and low.

"You wish," I spat back defiantly, pressing the balls of my feet firmly inside my stilettos and cementing them to the floor, my hands resting on either side of them.

He lowered his chin to his shoulder and peered at me from behind his shoulder. "Has it occurred to you I'm being nice?"

I blinked at him, the idea never entering my mind, but before I could give it another thought, shouting repeated around the penthouse. "Surprise!" Lourde chorused it first, with others echoing around her.

Everyone jumped up around me, causing me to lose

balance. With one quick hand, he turned and lifted me upright.

"Surprise!" I said weakly as he held me.

"I had that." I wriggled out of his hold. His touch burned on my forearm like a blue flame, and the warmth lingered from his large hands that swallowed me whole.

His eyes dragged down my body painfully slowly, and my breath caught in my throat. His gaze steadied on mine, and my body tingled with a betraying heat.

Yes, he's hot. Get over it, Olivia. He is also your boss and an arrogant jerk. You seriously need to get laid.

"Did you?" he questioned, raising an eyebrow, his velvet eyes never leaving mine. Commotion echoed around us with cheers and people obviously welcoming Evelyn and Barrett. But that all seemed a world away.

I stepped back, but instead of finding freedom and space, my back hit the concrete pillar.

Bringing my back ramrod straight, I bristled, then adjusted. I may not have intended to hit the pillar, but I was damn intent on making sure he didn't know that.

He stepped forward, closing the small gap between us. Electricity zinged between us.

Looking up, my gaze met his defiance yet caring eyes.

"I had that," I repeated.

He leaned down, closing the space between us. This close, I could make out the fine dusting of hair on his golden sun-kissed skin in his open-neck shirt, and I swallowed down the lump lodged in my throat.

His mouth to my ear, he whispered, "You wish you had that." His nose brushed the shell of my ear. My heart was thumping in my ribcage, wanting to launch out and be free from whatever this was.

Quickly, I pushed off the wall and past him, the sudden

Missing Love

feeling to flee overtaking all my senses. But I wasn't fast enough. He grabbed my wrist, and I turned.

"You might be God's gift to women, but your charms don't work on me, Ari."

He roared with laughter, a laughter that made others turn. I shook out of his clutch-like grip, aware of the eyes on us both.

My arousal had betrayed me, an ache pooling in my groin. I feared he sensed it too. Actually, I knew he did, the cocky son of a bitch. "You're a poor liar, Ms. Willows." His voice was gritty like sandpaper.

He stepped forward, keeping a space between us, and crooked his neck. Musky sandalwood filtered into my senses and awoke my lady parts. *Fuck.*

I rolled my eyes, but before I could walk away, he brushed past me, leaving me a shell of the woman I was when I walked in. I took a moment to gather myself, and, in particular, cool down.

The waiter offered me a drink when I stopped him, and I drank the champagne in one go. The bubbles slid down my throat, cooling my nerves. Taking a much-needed deep breath, I tried to reason with myself.

Okay, so whatever that was, it was fine because A, we weren't at work, and B, it was a normal reaction. The man was sinfully gorgeous, and I'm a red-blooded woman.

Normal reaction.

Completely.

Didn't mean I was going to act on the ache between my thighs.

The guy was still an A-class jerk and my boss.

And I'd forgotten about his lips on mine weeks ago. *Right?*

Heat warmed my chest, sending tendrils of warmth to the nape of my neck. When I looked up, I found Ari's stare upon me. Surrounded by a throng of models clamoring for his attention, he leaned against the table effortlessly, a smile forming on his lips as his stare cornered me.

Typical. Of course, women would worship the ground he walked on. Hell, I bet they'd line up to lay out a carpet of rose petals at his feet if he asked.

I rolled my eyes. To guys like Ari and Magnus, having women fawn all over them was perfectly natural, but I was damn sure not one of them and was more certain than the sun that I would not become another of his playthings, even with my body knocking on my door and wanting to betray me otherwise.

The champagne had relaxed me enough that I completely forgot about Ari for most of the night. I didn't even know what time it was, nor did I care as I was in hysterics at Pepper and Lourde making fun of the imposter who was posing like a bird and posting selfies of herself on the penthouse balcony.

"I think we should confiscate the phones of these girls," Pepper suggested, referring to said poser. She wrapped her arms around Connor's neck, and he nuzzled her cheek, whispering something in her ear, then her mouth tipped into a grin.

It was so great to see her with Lourdes' brother, and Lourde was so completely cool about it too. My besties were completely and utterly in love, and I couldn't be happier for them.

But part of me, the part I'd buried over the years, wondered if I could have it all too. If there was someone man enough to take all of me.

"Maybe if Ari vetted his model friends better, we wouldn't have to watch freeze-frame posing for an hour on the deck," Lourde said, interlacing her hands with Barrett's. Her engagement ring was beautiful and blinding when the light hit it.

"Magnus wanted women here, Ari just provided," Barrett said as we sat around the circular leather couch.

Our heads mirrored Barrett's as we watched Magnus in his element. A woman on each knee, he was lapping up his newly single life. Next to him, Ari sat legs apart, arms outstretched, drinking amber ale. I watched the gorgeous women surround him, reveling in his charm. The same charm he'd tried on me.

His words looped in my mind, and anger reared its head. "So nice for Ari to facilitate Magnus' needs, so does that make him his pimp?" They all laughed, but I didn't.

"Call it what you like, but the man always delivers," Connor said.

Pepper straightened, then elbowed Connor in the ribs. "There will be no more deliveries for you."

Connor held his hands up in surrender. "Cleary, I'm off the market," he said, then planted a possessive kiss on Pepper's lips.

Lourde scrunched up her face. "Okay, I said I'm cool with you guys, but you don't have to kiss in front of me," she said, recoiling, then grabbed the flute in front of her, the force sending the champagne spilling out.

"Like this?" Barrett questioned with a smirk, pulling Lourde into his arms, tilting her down over his knee and brandishing her with his mouth.

"Oh, hell no," Connor groaned out. "That's my sister, bro. Come on."

And my old boss... which, hey, I was used to seeing them like that now, so it didn't matter to me.

"Well, she's my fiancée," Barrett said, resting his forehead on hers after their public display of affection.

I stared at the glass coffee table, feeling like the third and very single, thorny wheel in need of inflating.

"Hey, guys!" Evelyn walked toward us with a drink in hand and a smile that could power the grid. Relief overcame me as her approach distracted the happy couples and eased my discomfort.

"Sis, come sit." Barrett shuffled, making room for his older sister.

"This has been so great," she announced as she plopped down on the couch.

"Were you surprised?" I asked. "Did you have any idea your brother was up to this?"

"I had zero idea!"

"I love that. You know, I never knew this side of your brother existed before he and Lourde got together. I only saw the demanding boss side, the baller."

"I can hear you, Olivia," Barrett said.

"Good!" I replied, and he chuckled before returning to his conversation with the others.

"He is a real sweetheart. He has always taken care of me. He has that other side too, the serious, take-no-shit boss side."

Hmm, I wondered if Ari was similar. At work, he gave Anna Wintour a run for her money at being the meanest son-of-a-gun to inhabit the planet, but here, he seemed different. Kinder was a stretch. But maybe he didn't hate me after all. I mean, he was even flirting. *Was that flirting?* God, I don't know. The haze of champagne had made the previous events slightly fuzzy.

"Lourde tells me your new design company landed its first big contract over at Farrah."

"Yes, I started this week. Shame, Ari's my boss," I said honestly.

"Why, is he a baller too?" Evelyn asked.

I laughed out loud—that and other things she didn't need to know about.

Overhearing our conversation, Lourde swapped places with Barrett.

"Remember what I said. Ari is complicated," she added, trying to placate me.

"Yeah, I don't see that." Inadvertently, my eyes glanced at where he was. He was already staring at me. Like creepy staring. *What the?* He couldn't hear our conversation from across the living room. No, don't be deluded, Olivia. Then why was he staring?

I stared back, that familiar heat rearing its head at his magnetic pull, and the others disappeared again in a blur of conversation around me. Like an invisible cord passing between us, his eyes fixed on mine. My skin hummed with that excitement it had earlier, betraying every logical thought in my intelligent brain.

"He is an asshole," I mouthed loudly and directly to him, hoping he could hear or at least lip-read. His eyes widened, and he immediately pushed off the table. Ramrod straight, his eyes burned with fury.

I blinked, realizing what I'd done, and immediately excused myself from Evelyn and Lourde.

"Nature calls," I churned out in a hurry, wanting to flee from his hold.

I just called my boss an asshole to his face. Fuck stick in a bucket. I was, hell, drunk.

I paced down the hallway, locating the guest bathroom. Slipping inside, I shut the door behind me. Thank God I was alone, the heavy pressure on my chest lessening.

With my back against the door, I exhaled the breath I was holding. Damn, why had I done that? Walking toward the basin, I watched the candlelight flicker back and forth, dimly lighting the powder room with ambient light. Quieter in here and a reprieve from the DJ's music, I could gather my thoughts.

Immediately the door flew open. Ari slid in, then quietly closed it behind him.

"Ari, get out!" I snapped, my anger once again rising.

He rested his back on the door. "No," he countered.

"I could have been sitting on the toilet."

"Well, you should have locked the door."

Okay, he had a point there. His gaze lowered from my bare neck to the swell of my breasts. An ache in my lady parts pressed, moistening the fabric of my panties.

Dear God.

"What do you want?" I asked. My leg, having a mind of its own, thrust itself out like Angelina Jolie. I folded my arms, which inadvertently pushed my cleavage up, and he sucked in his lips.

Did he like what he saw? No, he had models around him. *Don't be ridiculous, Olivia.*

"You called me an asshole."

"You got that." He stepped off the door. "Well, you are." My bravado didn't match my leg, which was now bordering on a wobble.

"I'm anything but to the people that know me." His voice was gentle and calm, eerily so that the hairs on my arms bristled upright.

"I seriously doubt that," I quipped.

"It is you who dislikes me."

"Dislike." I scoffed. "Now that's a pleasant word."

"Why?"

"You called my work plain when you know damn well it isn't."

"Do I?" he asked, stepping closer so we were only a shoe apart. "How can I know for sure?" His breath fell on my cheek.

"What are you doing?" I asked as the tall man cornered me with his broad shoulders and strong body.

My body was betraying me. It had only been a few hours since I saw stars, but now, here I was, wet and ready to go again. I needed a lover. Preferably not battery-operated. Fuck, it had been too long since a man had been in my bed. But I was always the one in control, not the man. If I wanted Ari, I could have Ari.

"You are an enigma, Olivia." He looked at me with confusion in his eyes.

And it beats the shit out of me why, out of all the men in here, I'm finding myself in a locked bathroom with you.

I swallowed down the lump in my throat, then titled my head up, so I exposed the column of my neck to him. "Go back to your harem of models, Ari," I said, pressing my hand on his chest, the only space now between us.

My thumbs brushed against the open skin of his shirt, and a tingle shot up my spine.

"I'll say it again. You're a bad liar, Ms. Willows."

I breathed out, and as my lips parted, he crashed his mouth onto mine. His hands fell around my waist and pulled me close. *Oh, God!* I let him in. He tasted of top-shelf whiskey and pure carnal desire. Hands clawed at my waist, pulling me into him. I felt his thickness all the way down my legs. Holy salami, he was huge, like the rumors huge. During our drunken kiss, I must have been too blinded by the alcohol to notice his size.

He groaned as I rubbed up against him, and the sound made me warm between my legs. His mouth left mine, and with one deft move, his hands gripped my waist and lifted me onto the marble bathroom counter.

Too long had felt like it had passed, but when his lips touched my neck, my body lit up, and my hands found his hair, dragging his head down my body. He sucked and nipped from my neck, down my front, then his lips found the fabric of my sweetheart cup. *Oh my God.*

A knock at the door pulled me from my near orgasmic state, and I immediately jerked back. Half-hooded eyes stared back at me with the same desire.

"Go away!" he yelled at whoever was on the other side of the door.

"All right. Gee," a voice sounded, then footsteps became lighter as they walked away.

He grinned as he looked at me, wanting to devour every inch of my skin. But it was too late. My head had kicked in.

This is your boss.

Stop. This. Now.

Do you want to go back to being no one and nothing?

"Stop," I blurted out, pushing him away.

"What?" he breathed out, confusion spanning across his eyes.

"Ari, please. I don't understand what just happened here, but it's wrong."

He clutched the erection in his jean pants. "Sweetheart, this is not wrong."

I cast my eyes down to his bulge. "No, that is certainly not wrong." I swallowed down the lump in my throat in an attempt to revert my attention. "There are a mountain of women out there that can fix that. I'm not a plaything," I quipped, then glanced at him briefly. He angled back, away from me, and I took that opportunity.

Grabbing my clutch on the counter, I quickly breezed past him, unlocked the door, and fled.

8

ARI

What the fuck just happened there?

I waited a few minutes for my bulge to go down.

She'd happily ignored me all night. From across the room, I'd studied her intently, but it was as though I didn't even exist, and the more the night went on, the more frustrated I became.

I had expected to see her tonight, and I didn't care. But when she appeared in that little black dress with the scarf wrapped around her waist, I imagined using it to restrain her. Her killer legs, short blonde bob, bright red lips... well, damn, she held my attention. More so than the supermodels next to me, and that didn't make an ounce of sense, especially since this was the woman who loathed me, and I didn't care if she got taken out by the mafia.

Then she'd mouthed the word 'asshole' directly to my face, and that was that.

All night she'd ignored me to then stare at me and call me an asshole?

What the actual fuck?

I was so tempted to rub one out in my best friend's bathroom, but instead, I flung open the door, frustrated as all hell, and stalked back to the party with the biggest blue balls known to man.

Walking into the living room, I tried to find her. But she was gone. It was more a feeling than a knowing.

She had run out of the bathroom as soon as her head kicked in, and the fear in her eyes told a story of a woman who wouldn't repeat the same mistake twice. So getting out of here and avoiding me altogether was, of course, what she'd do.

But I still tasted her on my lips. Bubble-gum fruity fucking delicious. Like kissing a teenager under the bleachers on a summer day, delicious.

I glanced over to where Magnus was surrounded by Bettina, Alexandra, and Victoria, three models and our company tonight. Lovely girls, pleasant enough, and all obviously gorgeous.

Walking over to the bar, I fetched myself a refill of whiskey and wandered around to the corner of the couch, where Lourde and Barrett sat beside Evelyn, who seemed to be having the time of her life.

"I was wondering where you got to," Lourde said, pulling on my jacket, so I sat on the empty seat beside her.

Connor and Pepper chimed in, "We are going to take off, guys." Connor not so subtly squeezed Pepper's ass, and she let out a giggle.

"You do that," I said, taking the whiskey to my lips for a large gulp. "Enjoy yourselves, kids," I commented. Since Connor and Pepper moved in together, Connor had been the happiest I had ever seen him. He hadn't complained about running the family media company, and he'd even been overly affectionate, something he never did before Pepper.

"Enjoy yourselves. Just do it anywhere but in my penthouse," Barrett said, tipping his chin down and tossing Connor a once-over glare.

Well, shit, I'd certainly be leaving Barrett in the dark about my kiss and run with Olivia in his tidy little powder room. If it weren't for the fucking interruption, he might well have had to redo the powder room, especially since I was seconds away from losing control.

"Bye, honey." Pepper bent down and kissed Lourde on both cheeks, momentarily pulling me from the image of Olivia on the countertop with her legs apart and full breasts threatening to spill out of her bra.

"Ari, looking handsome as always." Pepper winked, and I held up my whiskey, which was now running dry, saluting her. "What can I say?"

"Don't make his head any bigger. "Connor laughed. "Look, a trio of models awaits the king," Connor said, nodding toward a smiling Victoria.

I smiled back. "Magnus can entertain them for a minute."

"I bet he will," Barrett said, laughing.

"If you're not careful, Magnus will take all three." It was Lourde's turn to laugh now.

"Gosh, really?" Evelyn asked naively, staring at her brother, then me.

The truth was, he could take all three back to his place. Magnus was on a downward spiral since his divorce, and I had been there. It didn't bother me one bit if tonight Magnus had his fun.

I was still trying to comprehend my flaky disposition around the blonde vixen who infuriated me to the brink of wanting to wrap her lips on mine. Anger and lust, were they that different?

"Thanks so much for coming," Evelyn said to Pepper and Connor. "It's so nice to have spent time with you."

"And you too! You are so sweet." Pepper pulled her up for a hug.

Evelyn stepped back slightly, and Pepper let her go. Connor gave her a kiss, slapped me on the back, then they disappeared.

After a few more rounds of whiskey, I grew tired of watching Barrett and Lourde together. Wedding plans bounced around, and I was half listening, half ruminating about why my balls felt so heavy and if I should message Olivia.

At least with Evelyn here, my mind was occupied. I found out about her life in Boston. Treatment on her leg was ongoing from her injuries sustained when she was younger, and Barrett's pleas to have her move to Manhattan may work as she announced she would consider it, much to the delight of Lourde.

But now Evelyn was dancing, looking like she was having the best night of her life, and I was stuck here. Next to a couple so in love, it hurt like the emptiness of a cold bed.

I sucked down the last of my recently topped-up whiskey. I'd do anything to have that love again. That feeling had been ripped away from me in an instant.

And just like that, I was back in the car with Sophia.

"Ari, slow down, please. It's raining."
"Let me open her up just a little, Soph."
"Honey, no."
"It's fine, relax," I said, convincing her with a smile.
The road veered right ahead, and I floored it. The roar of the engine sounded from my new Lamborghini. She held onto the side, and I chuckled.
"I want my new fiancé to be around for a long time," she jested.
"Damn, I love it when you call me that." I peeled my eyes off the road and rested a hand on her knee. Her diamond sparkled brightly. I'd had it made, three carat solitaire diamond in a platinum band. It was perfect, like her.
"So do I." She placed her hand momentarily on mine before guiding me back to the steering wheel.

"It's really coming down now. Two hands on the steering wheel, please, Ari."

"Okay, okay. Just as long as my hands can touch you all night long."

She left out a soft laugh. "They definitely can."

I sped up, wanting to arrive home from our weekend away and continue between the sheets. Rain pounded down, the wipers doing their best to clear the flooded windshield.

I glanced over at her, and she smiled at me. It hit my heart like a bullseye hitting its target. Everything was perfect. I was engaged to the girl of my dreams and a career with my grandmama that was thriving.

"Ari, what's that?" she yelled, pointing up ahead.

I stared at where she'd pointed. "Fuck!"

A pothole the size of a small car appeared a few yards ahead. I immediately swerved the car. But it was too late.

"Ari!" Her piercing scream sounded, then silence.

"Ari?" A hand shook me.

I jerked, then took in my surroundings. Dancing bodies, a DJ playing beats, and the woman who was staring at me. "Victoria."

"Ari, are you okay? It looks like you've just seen a ghost."

I stood, unsteady on my feet, and reached for the back of the couch. "I'm fine." I grabbed her hand. "Let's get out of here." I wanted so badly to fill the hole in my heart for tonight.

She smiled, then took my hand into hers. "I thought you'd never ask."

* * *

Back at my apartment, I couldn't sleep. I'd fucked Victoria, and she left. We had fun, and that was that.

But the moment of togetherness with someone was gone as soon as it came, and there was that regret that followed.

But for the first time, when I was balls deep inside of someone, my mind went elsewhere. And strange as fuck, it went straight to that smart-mouthed blonde-haired Ice Queen. That's when I gave it my all, emptying everything I had into her in the shudder of an orgasm. I swear I saw Victoria limp out the door after we were done.

But it was how I imagined fucking Olivia, giving her exactly what she deserved and shutting that pretty mouth up. The thought of her screaming my name thrilled me to the bone. How much she would hate surrendering to me. And how I'd love it.

The weekend was filled with going through the mountain of statements I'd requested from Accounting. Trying to decipher the over-complex reports took most of Sunday, and still, I felt as though I'd made little ground into uncovering any anomalies.

When Monday rolled around, I couldn't understand my eagerness in wanting to see Olivia. I hadn't contacted her since the party at Barrett's penthouse, wanting to see if she'd reach out first. But she hadn't.

I'd tasted Olivia twice now, and it was just a kiss, nothing at all remotely like what I did to Victoria. But Victoria's taste hadn't lingered in my mouth. Her touch hadn't burned on my skin, and the thought of Victoria had definitely not kept me up for most of the weekend.

A knock pulled me into the now.

9

OLIVIA

He was my boss.
    He called my work plain.
    He was a womanizer.
I was a professional woman in my thirties.
I hated him.
He hated me.
Perfect.

Now, I was ready. I smoothed down my black dress—this one below my knees. Coupled with a silk blouse underneath and black pumps, I exuded an executive woman.

Vivienne, his assistant, wasn't at her desk, so this was the perfect opportunity to put all of this behind us. I knocked at his door.

"Yes." His voice was low and even.

I took a sharp intake of breath and slid the door open.

He looked up from his desk, and a smile tipped on his mouth, reaching his mocha eyes.

Was he happy to see me?

His suit jacket hung up behind him, and he sat with his chalk-white shirt sleeves rolled up, revealing his corded tanned forearms. Effortlessly gorgeous like the models that filled Farrah's building, his tousled hair was messy and pulled to one side,

"Ms. Willows." His timbre tone reverberated its way between my thighs, and I clenched them together. At least we were back to formalities. Perfect. Maybe he had an ounce of professionalism after all.

"Aristotle."

He picked up a pen and put the tip in his mouth. My gaze inadvertently lowered to his mouth before I quickly gave myself an invisible slap across the face.

"Your taste is still on my lips."

Oh, hell no. Shut it down.

"So that was a big mistake," I blurted out.

He stopped chewing on the pen. "Sit down."

"I'm fine standing," I said, holding my mark, the tip of my toe burrowing that little further.

"I said sit down."

He stared at me, and I glared back in defiance. But part of me wanted to agree, especially to the tone he set and how it was as though we were in the bedroom rather than his office.

"Do you have to object to every single thing I ask?" He raked a hand through his tousled hair, frustrated.

I watched the vein of his neck tick. It was probably a good thing we were back to annoying one another. It's what we did best anyway.

"I just came by because I don't want what happened to jeopardize anything I've worked so hard for."

"We are two grown individuals, Ms. Willows. We can do what we like outside of this office... or perhaps in it." He fanned out his fingers and ran his hand along the surface of his desk.

Oh God.

I swallowed down the thickness lining my throat. This was

getting out of control, but then why did my gaze drift to the surface where his hands rubbed back along the leather top? And why could I imagine myself bent over on his desk with his towering height taking me from behind?

"Ari, stop," I said in a stern voice that I didn't know I possessed until now.

"It's Aristotle," he said, matter of fact.

Rage bubbled in my veins. Did he really think I was one of the thousand others notched on his bedpost? A smile tipped on his mouth, and that sent my pulse sky-high.

"You are so arrogant," I let out in a whisper.

His eyes raised, but he hadn't seemed surprised. "And you think you know me. You forgot to throw in womanizer… playboy…"

"Well, that goes without saying. You treat women like—"

"Like they want to be treated," he bellowed, bolting upright, his office chair pushed back with force. He narrowed his eyes, and the darkness that hid behind them made me realize I'd hit some kind of nerve.

"I had no complaints from Victoria over the weekend when she screamed out my name. If anything, she was walking out with a delightful limp and a smile on her face."

He fucked someone after we kissed? A slight pang of disappointment ran through me. I shook my head as his comment sunk in. "You're revolting," I added.

"Are you jealous?" His eyebrows raised in a question.

"You wish," I fired back.

"Let me tell you what's more revolting, Ms. Willows." Ari rounded the office, coming to sit at the front of the table and leaned back with his legs slightly apart. I had a direct beeline to his groin.

The gap between us was smaller, but still, I held my line, glued, in case I crossed over to slap, kiss, or kill him. It was becoming a fine line at this point.

"The fact that when I was fucking a model, I was thinking it was you…"

I gasped in surprise, my heart becoming louder as it pounded in my chest, trying to comprehend what he had just said. But did he actually say that?

Now electricity was rife between us. Confused and taken aback, I just stared back at him, but I would not give Ari the reaction he was looking for.

No, that would be a win for Ari. Instead, I straightened my back and smiled.

"Wash that thought out of your mind because I guarantee you that will never *ever* happen."

He tilted his head to the side, amused. "I think you're forgetting that if I want something, I go after it, Ms. Willows."

"Well, lucky for you, the thought is revolting, right? You said it yourself, so you can go back to fucking your plethora of models and let me get on with my work. Because, believe me, if you want me to open this store in time, there is an endless amount of work still to be done." My voice came out strained. Elevated and in distress. And damn, if I was.

I watched his fingers curl around the edge of the table, but he stared at me in, what was that, confusion? He enjoyed seeing me like this, the sick sadistic, arrogant son of a bitch.

I cleared my voice. "Now, if you don't mind," I said, my legs finding their movement again as I turned around.

He said nothing, so I turned and opened his sliding doors. Feeling his eyes on my back, I swished my hips from side to side, my inner goddess wanting to rub in his face what he could never ever have.

I closed the door forcefully behind me and quickly called the elevator, seeking the solace of the four walls in my office.

My skin burned with rage. Thinking it was me he was fucking, then saying it was revolting? Why did I still hover on his lips, and why on earth couldn't I get said kiss out of my mind?

* * *

Half the week passed, and I received many emails from Farrah, first apologizing that we couldn't meet, then with the emails that followed, confirmation on the go-ahead for Plan C and the approval of my suggested supplier list.

Ari pushing me to make a Plan C, although a ball-ache at the time, proved to be the right move. *So what if he was right?*

Days blurred into one as I tried to source suppliers, budgets, and contractors to get the store ready and open in just two weeks. When Wednesday morning rolled around, I was sleep deprived, and I'd been delegating to my team so much, they also looked like they'd been burning the midnight oil. But even with Ari's resources, everything rested squarely on my shoulders.

Ari had left me alone for the last couple of days, which was a relief that we could just put this whole misunderstanding behind us. We continued as if nothing had happened. Emails were civil, and the handful of times I'd seen him, he had been bogged down in mountains of paperwork or in meetings.

Perhaps he did something after all.

There was the managerial style of letting me run with my autonomy. Then there was too much independence. And I got the feeling he was purposely ignoring me. The thought unsettled me, especially as I was about to leave on a road trip for the next two days to confirm two new suppliers for the store.

10

ARI

She'd ignored me since Monday morning, punishing me for the way she misconstrued what I'd said. Okay, so I'd kept my distance too, but with my workload the way it was, I thought it wise to get a grasp on it and steer clear of the woman occupying my mind.

You know what's more revolting, Ms. Willows? The fact that when I was fucking a model, I was thinking it was you!

Okay, now I can see how she took that the wrong way, especially when one word would have changed the meaning entirely. Instead of saying it was revolting, I could have said what I truly felt. It was surprising. Because heck it was. I didn't understand it. All I realized was when I was fucking a model, I wished it was Olivia. There was nothing revolting about that.

Shocking, I know, even for me to realize that. Obviously, coming back to work and plowing into pages and pages of accounts had frazzled my brain so much that the annoying Olivia had been plaguing my mind incessantly.

I even jerked off in the shower this morning, thinking of her. *What the fuck?*

But if she thought I was going to let her out of my sight for another two days, she thought wrong. Another assumption on her part to add to her never-ending Ari assumption tally.

I said goodbye to Grandmama and rode the elevator down one floor. Bypassing her team, who stared up at me from their workstations, I marched past them without uttering a word and into Olivia's office. I shut the door behind me and dropped my leather embossed overnight bag at the front door. A heavy thud sounded.

"Ari, what brings you down to the lesser floor?"

A chuckle escaped me. "That's the first time I've heard it called that."

"Well, there's a first time for everything," she countered.

"There is, isn't there?" I held her gaze and noticed a slight blush cloud her cheeks.

The undercurrent passed through her too, and it satisfied me knowing I had an effect on the Ice Queen whether or not she admitted it.

"You haven't gotten back to my many emails," she said, diverting her attention to her laptop to shut me out. Nice try, sweetheart, but it wouldn't work.

I walked over and sat beside her on the edge of her desk. She looked up in alarm before diverting her attention back down.

"I've been busy, princess," I added.

She blew out air, and a sneer sounded from the back of her throat.

Did she think I sat on a throne while being spoon-fed Beluga caviar by a model? *Fuck!*

Another assumption, another goddamn assumption. My skin blazed, and in an instant, she'd turned my calm temperament into an asteroid-sized fireball.

"Get up. We're leaving." I closed my fingers around her wrist, gripping her tight.

"We?" She looked up and blinked. Then her gaze flew past

me to the door where my overnight bag was. Her hand balled together in a tight fist. Her jaw stuck out as it dawned on her.

"You're not going alone," I instructed, the pads of my fingers pressed into the soft part of her skin. She hadn't moved.

"So you read my emails?"

"All of them. So I know you're just about to leave to go to Connecticut, then drive to New Haven to see some designer by the name of Rex Carmichael."

She sat back in her chair, and her wrist slid from my hold. She straightened, then tilted her head toward mine.

"Well, you would have also read that I'm going alone."

"If you think I'm letting you make these decisions without me, you've come to the wrong place."

She stood. "You've let me run this entire project. Why do you want to come now?" Pacing behind her desk and toward the art deco windows, her lips pinched together on her glossy fire-engine lips. The slit in her skirt opened, revealing her caramel thigh.

My hand twitched, begging to run my hand up and underneath, releasing her balled-up tension. I sandwiched my hands together, trying to get a grasp on these feelings.

"Because it's in the finer details where everything shines."

She stopped pacing, and I dragged my eyes to hers, not caring if she saw me eye-fuck her. I raised my eyebrows and challenged her to defy me.

"I can't guarantee I won't murder you on this trip, Ari."

A grin lifted onto my face. "Not if I kill you first."

"Ugh." She let out a sigh.

"Who knows, you might like my hands clasped around your throat."

She rolled her lips inward and sucked in a quick, shallow breath. "You're not letting up, are you?"

"Never."

Electricity passed between us as the silence stretched over a few seconds. Then she pushed her chair in and underneath the desk with force and threw her hands up. "Fine, you win. But I'm driving. I have a rental car in my name, and there is nothing you can do about it."

"Fine, Ms. Willows, but I've upgraded your budget rental to a Maserati. Do you think you can handle the torque on that?" I questioned with a smile twisting on my mouth.

"What… how?" She grabbed her leopard print bag on the shelving behind her and looped it over her shoulder. "I can handle anything." She swatted away a wayward blonde hair, clearly up for the challenge.

My dick twitched in response. I was looking forward to this.

Standing from the desk, I snatched her bag out of her hands, and reluctantly she gave it up. Then I walked to the office door, grabbed mine, and turned to her. "Well, come on, time waits for no one," I said, sliding out the door.

She uttered nothing else as we left work and picked up the car. The silence was anything but comfortable, proving this was going to be a long trip.

She could handle the Maserati, and shit, I had to control myself from having a Texas boner watching her glide the car along the freeway, slicing through traffic like a diamond cutter. Unafraid of the power the machine wielded, she accelerated with a lead foot and appeared to enjoy it too. I couldn't help but stare at her.

It wasn't often Olivia had a smile on her face. Her body was relaxed, and she wasn't biting back at my every word.

When we stopped at the gas station, I filled up the car while Olivia got out to stretch her legs. Then after I paid the attendant, I seized the opportunity to move in.

"What do you think you're doing?" she asked as I stood in front of the driver's door.

"Driving. Obviously."

"That wasn't the deal." She came to stand in front of me, her hands resting on her hips in a standoff I was expecting.

"Well, if you can move me away from this door, you can drive." I stood, folding my arms across my chest with my legs slightly apart. She blinked, her gaze dropping slightly before she leveled at me.

"I'll even make it easier for you." I stepped forward, closing the gap between us and inhaling a breath full of fruity strawberries, so she could push past me. Momentarily, my mind went to the lingering taste she possessively held over my lips.

I watched her swallow down as she tilted her head up to mine. With the column of her neck exposed down to her collarbone, it took all my restraint not to sink my teeth into the supple part of her neck.

"Ari, you're just being childish," she said but quickly tried to dart around me. Reading her like a map, I launched to the side quicker than a coyote, and she collided with my chest. I wrapped my arms around her body so she couldn't escape.

"Ari, let me go." She shrieked, and I leaned down, her hair tossing about as she tried to wriggle free from me.

"Is that what you really want?" I whispered in her ear, and her thrashing halted. As though reading my thoughts, she gazed up as I peered down. Enormous dark blue eyes stared back.

"Yes, it is." A tremble of a voice left her lips. Reluctantly, I let her go and opened the driver's side door, collapsed in my seat, and slammed the door shut. The Ice Queen was back.

The dress cinched above her knee when she sat, her thigh smooth and toned. My gaze drifted to her alluring skin more often than not as the car roared closer to our destination.

"Eyes forward, Ari," she said, this time catching me in action.

"No," I replied, seeking comfort in her discomfort. "You

might control everything else in your life, but you can't control me, Ms. Willows, and where my attraction lies."

She lifted her hand to her throat and rolled her lips together, letting out a sigh. "Models and wayward sex not up to standard?"

Her eyes dazzled in the dusk light, and like a lightning bolt, something struck me in the middle of my chest. Immediately, I pushed it away.

"Tell me, Olivia, why is it you only seek the casual companionship of men?"

She dropped her hand to the side.

"Sanella mentioned he saw you on a dating site, so I took it upon myself to look you up. What did it say, again?" I took my finger to my mouth for effect. "Casual is my style."

"No, that's not…" She ran a hand through her short blonde hair, tucking one side over her ear.

"You are extra flexible too," I added, recalling the image of her in the splits pose.

"That is p-private!" she stammered. "I was young, drunk, and—"

"You're a hypocrite, Ms. Willows."

"No," she said, holding her hand up. "That profile was put up a long time ago. My roommate put it up."

She had a roommate? Male or female? And why did I care?

"So you don't have casual hookups?" I pressed the accelerator while the thought of her with another man rolled over my stomach.

"There's a difference between me and you, Ari. I'm too busy for love. You clearly just don't care for it."

Anger erupted in my veins. I smacked the steering wheel, the force sending a blinding pain up my hand and wrist. I stepped again on the accelerator, the grunt of the motor pushing the car quickly forward.

"Ari, slow down. You're going to get a ticket."

"I don't give a fuck about a ticket. You think I don't care about women?" My voice roared over the engine, resentment metallic on my tongue.

"And you think my work is plain?" she yelled back at me.

I pressed the gas harder, pushing the car on the highway, gliding in and out of traffic.

The sky split in half, and the rain started sheeting down as if harnessing its energy from my flushed cold veins. The wipers automatically came on.

"You have this preconceived notion of me, Ms. Willows, but you don't even know me."

"It's not preconceived at all," she countered almost immediately, and my jaw ticked with a pent-up rage that was near uncontrollable.

I swerved to the side, barely missing the car in front of me.

In my peripheral vision, I saw her reach for the handle above the window. With her other hand, she gripped the seat. "Ari, what are you trying to do? Kill me?"

My pulse increased, and my skin turned clammy. Déjà vu hit me like a smack in the face, and immediately, I slammed on the brakes. Olivia lurched forward toward the windshield, and I extended my arm so it hit her chest and stopped her from propelling forward.

"*Ari, what the fuck!*" she screamed out as her back hit the seat with a thud.

Quickly, I killed the engine, undid my seat belt, and kicked my door open. Then, quicker than the flash that mirrored the sky, I ran over to her side, nearly hyperventilating in anticipation of what lay on the other side of the door.

I opened the car door and dragged her out so she was standing.

Was she okay? Had I hurt her, had she bumped her head on the glass?

She leaned against the car, regaining her balance. Frantically, I looked over all the parts of her exposed skin.

"Are you hurt?" I asked, my voice almost breaking into a quiver.

"What?" She looked at me in confusion, but I kept searching for blood anywhere on her.

"Are you hurt? Did I hurt you?" I said, touching her arm, looking for any sign of damage or split skin.

"Ari, I'm fine," she said, reaching out and touching me on my forearm.

The sound of my heartbeat thrashed about in my ears, and I drew in short, shallow gasps. The thought of hurting Olivia brought everything back with Sophia.

"Ari, look at me," she said in a stern voice and pulled my shirt closer to her. I examined her completely, but she reached up and grabbed my head, pulling it down so her eyes were nearly level with mine.

She stared at me, fear and confusion in her eyes. I struggled to catch my breath as her eyes willed me to slow down my panting.

"Ari, feel me," she said, placing my hand on her chest. I felt the rise and fall of her chest, the beating of her heart, erratic but beating strong. With the other hand, she placed it on her cheek.

"I'm okay," she whispered, trying to calm me. My eyes dragged down to hers as she pulled me closer.

My head dipped low so my forehead touched the tip of her nose. Willing my erratic heart to slow, I inhaled sharply before releasing my breath in a forced exhale. Her fingers fanned out on my chest and the warmth of her hand lingered over my heart, comforting me.

"Breath, Ari." I stared into her eyes, and my breathing slowed as every second went by.

The fear in her eyes was replaced with something else, something that burned a flame between us. With my free hand, I dragged her chin up. Her mouth, a breadth from me, tipped open. Her fruit scent trickled a spark that shot up the base of my spine, and there wasn't a damn thing I could do to stop what was coming next.

My hand rounded the nape of her neck, and I pulled her up to my lips. I dragged my lips across hers, and she opened wider, inviting me in. Our teeth clashed at the force of our kiss. Olivia slipped a hand into my hair as I pulled her to my chest, wanting to feel the warmth of her body against mine.

We devoured each other in a desperate spine-tingling kiss, only coming up for air when we'd run out. It was a moment too long. Desperate for her, I trailed her jaw with soft kisses. She tilted her head back and moaned at the connection, the sound reverberating through me. I sucked and circled the column of her neck with my tongue.

"Ari, we are on the side of a highway." She breathed out, her nails clawing at my body.

"I don't give a fuck," I growled out. I lifted her dress and pressed my hands into her peach of an ass, pushing her into my thickness that hung like a lead balloon.

She moaned and pressed herself into my length that was now straining against the zipper of my pants, then hooked a leg up on my hip, seeking more pleasure. The feeling of her massaging her clit against me had me feverish and brick-hard.

I looked around, and past a row of trees, a barn was up ahead, in the middle of butt-fuck nowhere.

"Come with me." I dragged her by the hand off the side of the road and into the overgrown meadow.

"I have heels!" She squeezed my hand, struggling to keep up.

I stopped and turned, planting my lips on her mouth, missing the connection and slightly fearful she'd change her mind. Then without warning, I bent down, wrapped my hands around her thighs, and lifted her off the ground. She let out a yelp when I threw her over my shoulder.

"Ari!" she cried out in laughter.

"Soon, princess, my name will be on your lips."

I kicked open the wooden door to the abandoned barn and set her down. The last of the sun streamed into the window, lighting up a pile of blankets on an old wooden stove. I shook one out and laid it down on the planks of wood.

Watching her watching me, neither of us said anything, neither of us understanding but needing whatever this was.

"Come here," I growled out. Impatient, I walked over the checkered blanket toward Olivia as she stepped forward. Then I pulled her close. My lips traced her neck, down to her breasts through her dress. Gently at first, then firmer. "You're too dressed for me."

She twisted her lips in a smile. "Fine." She reached behind her back and undid the zipper. It slid down her body to her thighs. After stepping out of it, she lifted and folded it as she looked for somewhere to place it.

God, she was strange.

Frustrated, I took it out of her hands and tossed it aside. She let out a gasp at my quick movement.

"You're too dressed for me," she repeated my words as I salivated, watching her stand there in a gray lace bra and thong.

I sucked on my lip. Fuck, she'd been hiding this all that time.

"Fine," I said, echoing her words earlier.

I slipped out of my pants and briefs, then undid my shirt, tossing them to the ground.

Her eyes gazed at my cock. Huge and engorged, it slammed against my navel. She stared at it with uncertainty behind her bright blue eyes.

"Yes, sweetheart, it's big, but I will inch my way inside you, bit by bit until you feel all of me."

"I can take it," she breathed out, stepping forward and wrapping her hands around my engorgement.

I hissed out a breath as her hands rubbed down my shaft, then circled my head.

A flash of warmth slashed my chest at the connection. "I will stretch you beyond words, Ms. Willows."

I tipped her head up and raked my tongue across her teeth as she opened for me.

We came to lie down, and I trailed my tongue around her bra strap. I pulled down her bra, and her firm tear-drop breasts sprung free, her rose areola erect and inviting. Grazing my mouth over hers, I toyed with her nipple, massaging it between my thumb and index finger, causing her to let out a moan. The sound sparked something inside me, and I released her mouth, moving to her delicious tits and taking her nipple between my teeth. She moaned louder this time and writhed beneath me in pleasure.

She reached for my cock, but I swatted her away. If her hands touched me again, I feared I'd come.

"Shhh," I said, my mouth hovering over the curve of her breast, then her navel, where my tongue lashed in and out.

I dragged my chin down so it rested on the fabric of her thong. With my teeth, I grabbed the thin strap and pulled it down, my fingers delving into her supple shaved folds. She moaned, tipping her head back as I filled her with my fingers.

The need to taste her became overpowering, and I removed my fingers, dipping them into my mouth, licking them clean. She gazed up at me, her chest rising and falling.

"Open for me, baby. I need to see you." Shifting down, I buried my head between her thighs.

I sniffed her scent. The smell was driving me crazy. Without warning, I spread her apart with my hands and circled her clit-boner with my tongue. Flicking back and forth, moans escaped her mouth, making my dick ache for her.

"Honey, this is just a taste," I said, this time filling her with my tongue. Deeper, I thrust my tongue inside her, tasting her completely. Fuck, she tasted so sweet.

"Ari." She hissed on a moan, and I knew she was close.

I alternated between her clit and her opening, circling and flicking my tongue against her clit in an aggressive assault.

Her legs writhed next to me, and her thighs quivered. My hands palmed her stomach, wanting her to absorb everything I was giving her.

"*Fuck!*" she screamed out as she came on my tongue. I swallowed her down, erupting in my euphoria, then kissed the inside of her thigh.

"Turn around," I commanded in a desperation unknown to me.

She did as I asked and rolled onto her stomach.

I got on my knees and reached for my trouser pocket. There in my wallet, I ripped out a condom and tore the foil packet open between my teeth.

"This may hurt a bit," I said as I sunk low, my cock resting between her thighs.

She turned to the side, and as I dipped the head of my cock in, I watched her for any reaction to stop.

"More." She breathed, and I smiled while dipping into her further so I was halfway in.

Fuck, impatience gripped me like a wetsuit, but I willed myself to slow down.

Soft and tight, she felt fucking perfect. She moaned, and the sound made me inch the rest of the way in. She winced in pain.

"Fuck, are you okay?" I asked, nervous I'd hurt her.

"Fine. I want it all," Olivia murmured, digging her nails into my arms.

I groaned out. Sinking into Olivia until I couldn't, I needed to claim her and leave my mark on her. I stretched her further, and she writhed in pleasure and pain. Deep inside her, the feeling of her fullness sparked a heat throughout my veins. Dipping in and out, I quickened my pace. Her eyes closed, and her hands balled into fists beside her head as she tipped her hips up, meeting me thrust for thrust.

I fucked her hard and fast. Absorbing her, I reached for the crown of her head and tipped her hair back so her back curved and her head and neck lifted off the floor.

"You like that, don't you?"

"Yes," she whispered, her voice awash with air.

I slapped her ass again and again as she moaned out in a whimper.

"You make me so mad, Olivia."

"So punish me," she groaned out.

I drew in a possessive breath. Finally, a woman who could match my needs.

I gripped my hand around her hair and pulled tighter, curling her head back more. With my other hand, I circled her throat, rubbing the column of her neck with my thumb and index finger.

"I'm going to make you scream, Ms. Willows. You hear me?" I said, closing my hand around her throat and applying pressure.

She moaned, her body commanding my every thrust. I squeezed her throat, and the color of desire stretched across her golden back.

"Ari," she screamed out, and I released my grip to a gentle hold. The hand holding her hair gripped her waist, my balls clenched high, and my stomach muscles tensed. I could no longer hold it together. I let out a groan, emptying myself into her.

All the pent-up frustration, the anger, the fire, the confusion, Olivia drew it out of me.

11

OLIVIA

Blown away by Ari's wonder stick, I rolled onto my back. I felt too sated to move while trying to catch a full breath.

Beside me, he was trying to do the same. My gaze lowered to his contoured stomach, rising and falling and dusted with black hairs I wanted to trace with my fingers all the way down to the curve of his V. Then I imagined enclosing my mouth over his entire eight inches. Not long and skinny but perfectly thick all the way from base to tip. He wielded the sinful three—looks, muscles, and an oversized cock that could rival some of the best porn stars in the industry, I would bet money.

The same sinful three I said I could ignore.

"What are you smiling about?" I asked as my gaze drifted back up to meet him.

"I told you I get what I want."

I rolled my eyes. I didn't want to tell him I didn't understand what happened when we were arguing up to the moment when he pulled me out of the car. A fear in his eyes like I'd never seen scared me, and I pulled him close, wanting to take that away from him. It was then that things changed. A longing came over me, a need to have him, no matter what the cost.

"Are you always this annoying?" I sat upright, twisting to stand, then began searching for my clothes.

"Where do you think you're going?" He growled, reaching out for me and wanting me to lie back down next to him.

"We are late for our first appointment."

"Are you being serious right now?" He almost laughed in disbelief, but it was his tone that momentarily stopped me from zipping my dress.

"Of course," I uttered, resenting the professionalism that came over me like a mechanical watch. "While we're on the serious train, what happened to you before when you pulled me out of the car?"

He shot up, his muscles quickly jerking into action as he snatched up his shirt and trousers. "Nothing. Nothing at all. We don't want to be late." He yanked up his pants, then whipped on his shirt, quickly buttoning it up.

Damn. I didn't mean to make him mad. I had not intended for any of this. This situation was so screwed up, and the only way I knew how to deal with it was to turn back into my go-to control and professionalism.

It's what I knew. I couldn't jeopardize a fling for my livelihood, my parents' livelihood and future. I'd been paying off their mistake for the last decade, hoping they could retire and own their house.

No. I looked around the barn. It was pretty and quaint. Simple with one window, a few cobwebs in the corner, an old chair, a dusty table, and rickety weathered floor boards that had stood the test of time. The black and red checkered blanket where we lay moments earlier was still there, and the images of what went on filled my brain, making me ache between my legs.

Wanting more so soon? What was wrong with me? So what if he was the best lover I ever had? He was my boss, for Heaven's sake. And a womanizer. And I had a job to do.

I heard Ari toe into his shoes, and I dashed out of the barn. When I reached outside, the dusk light had morphed into a gray-blue, and I could just make out the Maserati about a hundred yards ahead of me. I set off toward the car, cursing myself with every step I walked away from him and toward the road.

Was I crazy for wanting him so badly? No, I was human. But my lack of control around him? That scared me the most.

I trudged through the field, the long grass grazing my ankles. The way in was a lot more enjoyable, but then again, I was hanging upside down over his strong shoulder with his hand on my ass.

I turned around and found him walking behind me. When his eyes met mine, I spun around and continued walking. Because what? Were we meant to walk together, like two lovers wandering in a field, holding hands and singing Lionel's "Endless Love?"

No.

There were no happy-ever-afters for workaholics like me, and definitely not the Ari's of the world where women were on rotation like the days of the week.

I slid into the passenger seat and smoothed down my dress, waiting for him to get in.

He slammed the door shut, and set the navigation to the meeting point we were already late for. An awkward silence descended upon us, and as we rode in silence through the darkness, I was the first to crack.

"I've contacted Rex Carmichael and said we had car trouble."

"Fine." His hand wrapped around the base of the steering wheel, his knuckles stretched paper-thin.

I cleared my throat. "Fine." Another pause.

And thank hell he floored it because, in under ten minutes, we had arrived at the address Rex had supplied. Weathered timber gates and a crooked wood sign bore the name *Carmichael Designs.* Beyond that, an overgrown garden and pathway meandered toward a quaint red shingled roof cottage.

Then there was my boss, who peered out of the windshield like he'd arrived in a third-world country.

"And we couldn't find this in Manhattan?" His tone dripped with sarcasm as he lowered his window and pressed the gate buzzer.

"Olivia?" A cheery voice greeted us on the other side.

"Aristotle and Olivia are here to see Mr. Carmichael."

"Call me Rex and wait right there. I'll see you in a jiffy."

"A jiffy?" Ari returned his gaze to me. "And have they heard of gate automation? That house is over two hundred yards away."

I rolled my eyes. "Perhaps it's not in the budget of an up-and-coming wood crafter."

He let out a groan, and my gaze fell to the modest house up ahead, trying to ignore his arrogance and snobbery.

A few minutes of silence passed when a man appeared in the light. Brawny and tall, he wore a backward Yankees cap and coveralls streaked with paint.

"You're kidding me." Ari let out an arrogant laugh and snap, just like that, we were there again. Like he controlled my body, Ari crawled his way under my skin, igniting me with anger.

The gate creaked on its hinges, and Rex held his hand to his forehead, shielding the bright light from the headlights. He stood to the side and waved us through.

"You know what, I think I'll walk." Without waiting for a reply, I unclipped my seat belt and pushed the door open, grabbed my satchel, and gave it a tug. When it didn't budge, I turned to find a smirk on Ari's angular jaw.

How did I just have mind-blowing sex with this man? The same man I now wanted to claw his eyes out.

Anger whipped through me like an inferno, and with one frustrated pull, I yanked the bag. It slid out from underneath the seat, smacking the dashboard as it flung through the air.

I took in the mark on the dashboard and shrugged. "Good thing you can afford to fix that."

I slammed the door shut with an almighty force and rushed in front of the stationary car, stopping a few yards ahead where Rex rested by the gate.

"Olivia. Welcome, thank you for coming." He stepped forward, and up close, I took in his arm, where tattoos snaked up his bicep, and his large blue eyes that smiled when they met mine.

"Sorry again, we're late," I added, momentarily blindsided by the handsome face shining back at me.

"No need to apologize. Things happen. Now let me help you. The ground is uneven there." He quickly appeared by my side, his hand finding its way to the small of my back as I navigated through the rocky driveway to find a flatter surface.

The engine roared behind me, and I immediately leaned into him as he led me up the driveway, leaving Ari to watch us both.

A roar sounded again, this time louder than before.

He could wait.

"I think he wants to come in." Carmichael laughed, and his hand left my back to wave him through.

I wondered if he was jealous. Good, I wanted to frustrate him like he had me.

I shook my head. *Keep your mind on the appointment, Olivia.*

Ari was already at the front entrance when we arrived. Acutely aware of his presence and his possessive eyes, I continued my conversation with Rex Carmichael about the historic cottage, trying not to be pulled into Ari's hypnotic and destructive power struggle.

"Ari Goldsmith," he said, his hand outstretched, not caring he'd interrupted us.

Rex's focus shifted to Ari. "Thanks for coming. I can't wait to show you what I've prepared."

"Me too," Ari replied, his normal gravelly low voice an octave higher than usual. If you didn't know Ari, you could have sworn he was being genuine, but he was anything but.

"And don't worry about being late. Us country folk don't stick to schedules like you city folk." He let out a chuckle before adding, "Olivia mentioned the car trouble?"

Ari brushed past me, walking ahead and ignoring me as he marched toward the studio behind Rex.

"Yes," Ari said.

"It must have been a bother changing the wheel," Rex commented as he swung open the barn door.

"It was a bitch," Ari stated, tilting his head over his shoulder and toward me.

That asshole! Was he seriously calling me a bitch? But I had called him an asshole to his face…

"Expensive cars really are overrated," I said and jutted my chin forward, keeping in step close behind him.

Ari stopped abruptly, and I nearly walked straight into him. He turned and faced me, his eyes dark and firm, held mine. I swallowed hard, unsure of what would come out of his mouth and doubted I could control what would come out of mine.

"Perhaps you should look under the hood one day, Ms. Willows."

Why? Besides your arrogant, womanizing ways, there's isn't that much more to you, Ari.

Rex had stopped now and was looking between us. Uncertain how to respond, I smiled nervously at Rex while my heart thumped loudly inside my chest. Ari stood glued to the floor, his gaze piercing bullet holes in my armor.

"Um, so, let me show you the cabinetry handles first," Rex spoke, and shit, was I relieved.

I nodded in his direction, encouraging him to continue, and he twisted his lips into a what-the-hell's-going-on-here smile.

Damn, were we that obvious?

"Perfect," Ari answered, whipping his head around and following Carmichael into the small room behind the studio entrance.

After my heart returned to its normal rhythm, I noticed the beauty of the small studio. White paneled walls and thick wooden shelving, all in different sizes, held his precious wooden designs.

Wow. These were truly beautiful pieces, and because Rex wasn't well known yet, he was at a fraction of the price of Manhattan suppliers.

But it wasn't necessarily the price that caught my eye, but the attention to detail. Wood in every species, dark woods, mahogany, and light oaks were expertly molded into half crescents and interesting organic shapes I'd never seen before. Baby smooth, then lacquered in different finishes, I marveled at the display.

However, it was the display to the right of the room that really caught my attention.

Wood coat hangers hung on an ornate rod like artworks in their own right.

"These," I said, walking over and picking one up, feeling the smooth hardwood between my fingers. The soft scent of wood, earthy and organic, a perfect match for Farrah's upcoming fall collection of forest greens and emerald color pallet.

Ari appeared beside me. He touched the same coat hanger

I held between my fingers. His hand accidentally brushed mine, bringing me back to us rolling around the barn floor, the chemistry that was undeniable not so long ago. I sucked in a breath at the connection, then quickly let go of the hanger, trying to shift my focus to another design in front of me.

"These are stunning," I said, my voice slightly hoarse. I cleared my throat, determined to keep whatever professionalism I had left.

"Rex, all of this..." I spun around the room, "... are works of art."

"That's kind of you to say." When my gaze found him, his eyes were already on me. A blush crept up on my cheeks. Goddamn, was it hot in here, and why did I feel like Ari was shooting arrows in my back?

"I have so much more. Let me show you," he shared with a wide smile, and I smiled back.

Rex walked ahead to another room toward the rear, one I hadn't noticed until now. I fell in step behind him, then felt a strong, possessive hand from behind curl around my elbow.

I turned around to find Ari invading my personal space.

"Stop it," he commanded through a tight jaw.

"What?" I breathed out. His eyes cursed me with each pounding heartbeat.

He tipped his head down, so his mouth brushed my cheek. "If you don't want me, fine. But flirt in front of me again, and you will pay, princess."

"I'm not flirting!" I hissed out, and Rex made a noise up ahead. Thankful he wasn't close to us because I felt my control shifting beneath me.

Ari narrowed his eyes, pulling me closer to him, his scent awakening my lady parts. His gaze was murderous in its intent.

"Okay," I offered meekly and damn, possessive much?

* * *

The meeting was a raging success. Everything Rex Carmichael designed was perfectly suited to the new store, and with Ari's nod of approval, I ordered everything we needed, making Rex Carmichael one very happy man. And busy. He had to make more than he had available and finish it in time for the store opening.

By the time we got to the hotel, I was positively exhausted and emotionally and physically spent, so when Ari called ahead and changed my booking at the local Inn to the fancy five-star boutique lodging, I didn't argue. I was thrilled. Although telling him that would be candy to his lips, and I wasn't giving him what he wanted. He got that from all the other women on their knees.

Modern but character-filled, my suite had a living room with a comfortable armchair and an office where I could attend to my never-ending emails. A huge flat-screen television was set into the wall, offering the latest movies. But the mini-bar, it was stocked with everything a single girl needed to enjoy a night in.

Which was exactly what I'd do after I called Mom. "Darling! Your father and I have been so worried."

"Sorry, Mom, just busy with work."

"How is it all going?"

I had told Mom and Dad about working for Farrah Goldsmith, leaving out the part of boss-hole, Ari Goldsmith.

"It's exactly what I thought it would be," I lamented. *Well, except for the part where my boss has the biggest cock I've ever seen and knows just how to use it.*

"Is it that bad?" Dad chimed in, cutting through my mental picture.

Ever since they discovered the ability to put me on a three-way conversation, they did.

"Yes, Dad, but nothing I can't handle." I smiled.

"That's my girl."

"Did you get the money I transferred last week?"

"Yes, thank you, darling, but how many times have we said to stop? You need to take care of yourself, Olivia, not your old parents."

"Mom, I will not rest until we pay the debt back, and you can have a house that no one can ever take from you."

"You're going to kill yourself trying," Dad said, and I could tell he was shaking his head at me.

"Dad's working double shifts now driving the bus, and I've picked up some shifts at the local Walmart. We will pay it back in no time," Mom said.

"Perhaps it would have been if the rich prick hadn't charged you an exorbitant interest rate and scammed you into a deal that was too good to be true."

"Now, now, we've been through this before. We can't be angry at our past mistake, Livvy."

"Why not! Guys like that should be in jail."

"Yes, well, I can't argue with you on that one."

A knock sounded at my door, and I quickly slipped up off my bed, pulling my satin gown closed.

"Is someone there?" Dad asked.

"Yes, I'm just on a work trip, and someone's at the door."

"Dinner when you get back?"

"I'd love that," I said quickly, walking to my suite door.

"Bye, beautiful. Promise me you'll rest up?"

I'll rest when I'm dead and when I know you are okay.

"Of course, Dad. Bye."

I opened the door, and there staring back at me was Ari in nothing but a towel, the tips of his hair dripping with water.

12

ARI

Damn crazy Ice Queen. She drove me mad. One minute she burned for me, and the next, she was ice cold.

Then at the meeting with Rex Carmichael, she bordered on the edge of flirtation with a guy who could double as Brad fucking Pitt.

No. Not on my watch. Not happening.

Any which way I played it out on my mind, it was a roundabout of clusterfucks and confusion. Not only had I feared the worst when I slammed on the brakes of the Maserati, but there was a look in her eyes, a glimpse into the real Olivia, and a vulnerability that dialed back my racing heart rate to its normal rhythm. Behind all the work pretenses and walls, she cared for a moment. She showed the same vulnerability I recognized in myself once upon a time when I let my heart be open to such a thing.

But then, that coupled with a desire to leave the barn as soon as we fucked, and I just couldn't get her out of my mind.

Enough so that I slammed the tiled wall of my suite while

in the shower, angry at her for making me this way and determined not to let her affect me that way again.

Yes. I'd tell her exactly what was on my mind. Get it off my chest so I could at least sleep tonight. And not ruminate.

When she opened the door, her gaze momentarily dragged down to my chest, then back up to my eyes. *Look all you want, sweetheart, because the more you fight me, the more I want you.*

I affected her whether or not she admitted it.

"Clothes too tight around those muscles of yours?"

"Shut that pretty mouth of yours and listen."

Her eyes widened like dinner plates. "I beg your pardon," she snapped, pulling her satin robe closed.

"You heard me," I said, walking into her suite and leaving her to shut the door behind me.

Her suite was the mirror image of mine, except she had already set up her computer and folders on the desk in the corner—ever the workaholic she was.

"What is it, Ari? I'm tired." She walked to where I stood.

"*What is it?* You can't be serious?"

"Deadly. I have zero idea why you are in here, dripping wet too, might I add."

I looked down. Damn, had I rushed out that quickly without even drying myself? See? The woman drove me bonkers.

"Why did you flirt with him after what we did in the barn?"

"I didn't flirt with him," she protested.

"Bullshit. You did it in front of my face."

She paced the small room, back and forth, feeling the discomfort of my inquisition. *Good.*

"Did you want to know if I feel anything? Is that it?" She laughed, and I raised my eyes in a question.

"Fuck, and here I was thinking I was the one messed up," I said, wondering how such a beautiful, intriguing, and painfully annoying woman like Olivia wasn't hitched.

"I'm n-not messed up," she stammered in a wounded voice, and I knew I'd hit a nerve. She leaned against the wall and sandwiched her arms over her robe.

"Then why did you leave as soon as I made you come?" I stared at her. "What are you afraid of?"

Her jaw relaxed, and she shifted, but I'd sent her off-kilter, and it took her a moment to collect herself. "Nothing and no one, especially you."

"Liar, Ms. Willows." I stalked closer toward her like a predator squaring off its prey.

"I think you're afraid of me. I think every time you see me, you want me like I want you."

Another step.

"Painfully so, like a confusing addiction," I added.

"Ari." Her voice held soft. She raked her teeth across her bottom lip, her head tilting to look at my damp chest, then back up to meet my stare. My half-hooded eyes stared back at her. "This is not a good idea."

"I agree with you there."

She blinked, her breath hitching in her throat.

"But there's something about you that draws me in." I ran the back of my hand down the lapel of her satin robe, along the curve of her breast. Momentarily, she closed her eyes, drawing in a breath. Hard erect nipples pushed against the satin fabric, and desire shot through me.

"Jesus, I hate you." She went to slap my hand away in a playful swat, but I captured it in mine. Wrapping my fingers around hers, I bent down, closing the gap between us.

I brushed her lips, begging her to open for me. I needed to taste her again.

My prayers were answered as she did almost immediately. Teeth clashed and tongues collided in an all-consuming kiss that had my veins pumping with adrenaline. I pushed my body up against hers possessively, wanting to feel all of her on my skin.

Then I grabbed her hands and raised them above her head, holding them with one hand as I reclaimed her lips. "Hate is a strong word, Olivia," I whispered in her ear while nipping at her jaw. She let out a moan and tilted her head back against the wall, lengthening her neck.

Dragging my mouth to her skin, I traced the line of her jaw and down the side of her neck with heated kisses. She moaned at the connection, and the sound had me wanting to please her more.

With my other hand, I tugged on her belt, loosening it, and slid open her robe. Dressed in tiny satin shorts and a thin camisole that showed the outline of her breasts and nipples, my dick swelled underneath my towel. Her natural body was a sin sent to kill me. I was sure of it.

She kept her hands high above her head when I let go to undress her. First, the shorts. My thumbs circled the seam, brushing her waist teasingly. Then slowly, I pushed them down her legs, my hand trailing the backs of her warm thighs down to her ankles. I looked up to find she was staring at me. Then she stepped out of her shorts, but I didn't move, frozen in her gaze.

Naked from the waist down, all control I thought I had, went out the window.

"Open for me," I commanded as I sank to my knees, my towel notched loosely around my hips. "I need to taste you."

She did as I asked and parted her legs. With both hands on her thighs, I pushed her open further, inhaling her scent before I plowed inside her tight folds. Ready and wet, she tasted like Christmas in a cup.

I heard her suck in a breath and gripped her ass, driving her closer and wanting to give her exactly what she craved. Exactly what she was fighting. Coming up for air, I circled her clit and pushed my fingers inside her. She was dripping wet, and I groaned out, the sound reverberating on her clit and sending her moans into overdrive. Entering two fingers inside, I stretched her. Then, in and out, with the windmill rhythm of my tongue relentless against her clit, I devoured her.

I gazed up momentarily, watching her lose all control. With her head to the side and her eyes shut tight, I knew she was close as she clenched around my fingers.

I peeled my mouth away from her, leaving my fingers inside her.

"Open your eyes and watch me feast on your cunt while I make you come."

She snapped open her eyes, and I went back to working her delicious clit. Wanting to make her throb hard, I continued my punishing assault.

"Ari." She breathed out, her diaphragm expanding and contracting as her breath shortened. Olivia's hands fell into my hair and fisted it between her fingers, nearly pulling it out with her strength.

I drew back for a second and blew on her clit, before taking it again and sucking it between my lips. I stared up at her, lips apart, blue eyes dark. "*Ari!*" she screamed out, and the sound had a smile playing on my lips and a warmth feeding my legs all the way up my spine.

I licked her off my lips, my body humming with the insatiable thirst to have her. Then pushing off on my toes, I wrapped my hands around the back of her knees, hoisting her into the air. Her hands fell around my back as I flipped her over my shoulder. "Seriously, Ari, what are you doing," she protested.

I stood and slapped her bare ass, her pussy hot against my shoulder as I walked from the living room into her bedroom. Then standing at the side of the bed, I swung her over and gently dropped her in the middle of the bed.

"I'm not a little thing you can just throw around!"

"No, you're a smart-mouthed woman who drives me crazy," I said as I stared down at her.

She flung off her camisole and got on her knees.

"This smart mouth?" She leveled herself with my towel, then gazed up at me with heavy-set doe eyes.

My hands gripped her jaw. "Don't tempt me, Olivia, not if you're not going to do something about it."

She smiled, then found the knotted end of the towel and released it. The towel fell on the carpeted floor, and I stood there with my dick sky-high and thick against my torso. I dropped my hands from around her chin as she grabbed my dick with both hands, lowering it into her mouth. I hissed at the connection of her warm wet lips around the rim then she closed her lips around me, dragging her mouth down my long shaft.

Oh, holy shit.

She took all of me in her mouth and down her throat. I swallowed, feeling the bob of my Adam's apple in my throat. "Fuck," I groaned out in awe. Not many, if any, had taken all of me before. I gazed in wonder, watching this blonde Ice Queen burn for me like I did for her. I placed my hand in her hair, more for support than anything else. Because damn, the girl had skills. She ran her tongue along the base of my cock, and the sensation drove me wild.

She took me again, this time gagging as she pushed me further down her throat.

"Olivia. I don't want to come in your mouth, but fuck if you keep doing that…" My voice trailed off, and it was as though she couldn't hear me. She moaned around my cock.

Oh God.

She gave my balls a gentle, firm massage, again gliding up and down my dick with her moist wet lips. A second later, she gagged around my head as she came up for air, then continued her manifesto on my dick.

She looked up through thick lashes, and fuck, I was done for. "Olivia!" I hissed out, and instead of backing away, she sucked me harder. I pulsed into her mouth hard and fast, her eyes not straying from mine. She swallowed me down, then wiped her mouth with the back of her hand and fell back onto her hands.

"Jesus Christ," I said, filling my lungs with air before speaking again. "I should have known that smart mouth could take my enormous cock."

A smile played on her mouth, and there it was, that glimpse into the real Olivia. If it were only for a moment, I'd take it.

"Why, thank you," she said, her gaze holding mine.

"How many lovers have you had?" I asked, knowing I was heading into personal territory and one we hadn't crossed before.

"Boyfriends, a handful. Lovers, a few more than that."

I ran a hand through my hair. "Why only a handful of boyfriends?"

I wanted to hurt, maim, and destroy every son-of-bitch she'd even been with.

"Oh, you know…" Her voice drifted off. "I think some men are threatened by me."

Her gaze dragged up to meet mine, and something inside me tugged. There she was, the real Olivia, the one I wanted so desperately to see more of.

"But not you, Ari. Your womanizing ways have you firmly in control, don't they?"

… and just like that, it was gone.

"Don't," I said in a firm but gentle voice.

"Don't what?" she asked wide-eyed.

"Do this. Minimize what we just shared to nothing at all." She let out a nervous laugh, and if she thought I was going to stand here and listen to her ruin another moment we had, she thought wrong.

Bending down, I reached for my towel, sliding it around my waist, then tied it into a knot, pulling the ends tight so they clung to my hips. But in the time it took me to wrap myself in a towel, Olivia still had said nothing in response. I let out a sigh. Normally, I could understand women, but Olivia was an anomaly I couldn't work out.

"Where are you going?" she asked, wrapping her arms across her knees after pulling the sheet over her body.

"Back to my room unless you want me to sleep here?" I inquired, inviting her to let her guard down and secretly hoping she would.

"What's the point in having two rooms then?" Any hopes I had disappeared in an instant, and a pang of disappointment flooded through me. Surprised that my feelings for his woman had shifted into something other than hatred, I decided it was time to leave.

"Good night, beautiful." I leaned down, kissing her on the forehead in a move that even took me by surprise as much as it did her. She looked up at me, confusion stretching across her smooth skin. A light dusting of pink clouded her sun-kissed cheeks, and she opened her mouth to speak.

"Night," she said, clearing her throat and slinking further into the covers. "Don't forget to set your alarm. We can't be late for another meeting."

I flared my nostrils and turned my back. All hail the Ice Queen. She was back and frozen solid.

13

OLIVIA

Well, that was certainly not what I expected or wanted.
Until I wanted it.
More than anything, I wanted to please him like he had me. Craving to touch him, to have him in my mouth and show him I wanted him without words. Words I failed at miserably, but my actions spoke volumes.

He read my body, controlling me like a conductor with his proteges. And I let him. Unable to control myself, I submitted to him. Both my body and mind were his, and for the time we were intimate, separation blurred. I was out of my head and taken away, and from his possessive touch and throaty groans, I could tell he was too.

I'd never had the insatiable urge to please a man. But with Ari, it was different. Maybe it had to do with the awe and fire behind his eyes when he looked at me. He held that same craving so deep and desperate that I did.

And I couldn't understand it.

Because I was affected by the man I loathed.

The man who made me flush equally with both anger and desire.

I hadn't slept that soundly in forever. So when my alarm sounded, it scared the living daylights out of me, and I jerked upright, tossing my covers to the side with the movement.

I'd washed myself countless times in the shower, thinking incessantly and trying to make sense of what had transpired in the last twelve hours. You could eat sashimi off my foot, it was that squeaky clean.

Yet with all the thinking, it still made little sense. Ari? Me? None of it. All I knew was I was fighting a battle, one that was slipping through my fingers with each wayward glance he shot at me.

We flew through the meetings and were minutes away from the Manhattan exit when the conversation turned from the store opening to something more personal.

"Tell me about your folks," he asked, keeping his gaze firmly ahead.

"They're amazing. Both hard-working parents living the American Dream."

"Only child?"

"Uh-huh."

He turned and smiled, his boyish eyes catching a finger of light and making my breath hitch in my throat. "Same."

"Tell me about yours?" I countered, wanting to know more about him and less him learning about my poverty-laden past.

"My mom, Deidra, and dad, Spencer, have never had to work a day in their life. Much like me in the last ten years anyway." He looked over at me, but it didn't feel like he was saying it out of arrogance. But he was checking in on me, searching me for a response.

"Go on," I encouraged, holding back my normal snarky response.

He smiled. "Mom loves to cook Spanish food, and Dad builds model cars. They have a great relationship."

"Spanish food?" I inquired.

"Don't ask." He laughed aloud, and my shoulders relaxed at the sound.

"Okay, so model cars?"

"Dad loves it. When they're not living in Monte Carlo, he spends all day in his hobby room, then comes out for Mom's amazing Spanish food at dinner."

I watched him talk about his parents. His face radiated as he spoke of them, and it reminded me of the strong relationship I had with mine.

"They were never interested in working with Farrah?"

"No. Never. And Farrah never asked her daughter to follow her. She always wanted her to do her own thing."

"I see. They sound wonderful."

"Yeah."

It took the silence for me to fill the space, curiosity getting the better of me. "So are you going to tell me what happened yesterday when you pulled over suddenly and freaked out on me?"

He glided the Maserati onto Third Avenue, appearing to contemplate my question.

"I think I've answered enough questions for now. Don't you?" He glanced at me, a slight smile edged up from the corner of his mouth.

I twisted my lips into a smile. "For now."

He held my stare, and damn, the air was stifling. Nervously, I rolled my lips in and on themselves, fidgeting with my hands in my lap.

"Don't think you're getting away from me that easily, Olivia. You may have avoided my questions today, but you know as well as I do when I want something, I get it, and right now, I want you."

"You are persistent, Ari."

"And you love it."

My gaze drifted outside. Sunburst clouded my vision as a tingling sensation spread across my chest outward. "So full of yourself," I countered.

"And you love being full of me too." He smirked.

I split into laughter. I couldn't help it.

"So…" he said, the word lingering in the air as we pulled into the parking garage of FGC.

"So, we have achieved a lot. Everything is on track for the opening Friday week. And I will work my ass off to ensure it runs smoothly. You don't have to monitor me, Ari."

He pulled the car into a tight spot, expertly gliding it in at a fast speed that had me holding my breath until he killed the engine. Then he slid out of the car and hurried to my door, where he opened it for me, his gentlemanly gesture taking me by surprise.

"Well, we didn't kill each other," he remarked, his eyes looking down at my body as though I was wearing nothing at all.

I blushed. Since when did blushing become the new normal for me?

Holding the hand that he held out for me, I stepped out. His hand firmly clasped around mine, the warmth radiating up my arm.

"Not yet." I smiled back at him, and a flicker of hope sprung in his eyes.

Not that I meant it like that. This was a once-off thing, wasn't it? He knew commitment like I knew how to relax. Hardly at all.

I quickly corrected myself. "What I mean to say is that this was fun, but that's all. I'm busy with work, and you're busy with… whatever it is you're busy with." I pulled my bag over my shoulder and walked ahead of him, feeling his presence close behind me.

An uncomfortable silence descended, and when I reached the elevator, I turned around feeling unsettled.

"Say something," I said. "It's not like you to not say anything."

"You're probably right," he agreed. His gaze hit me, and there was a resignation behind his eyes. Wait, what was that look? Did that mean he wanted this? Wanted *us*?

It didn't matter what he wanted. I was too busy for love. Too busy to jeopardize everything I'd worked my ass off for some fling in the night. If I focused on him and us, I was bound to make a mistake, let my new business fall to the wayside and be back to square one.

I couldn't do that, I had to bail my parents out of their hell-hole financial troubles, and I had a responsibility to myself to see this business through to a burgeoning start. And shacking up with an arrogant womanizer wasn't the way forward, especially since there was a hidden promise of revamping all FGC's East Coast stores if this one hit the mark.

Except everything inside me screamed for his touch again.

"Agreed," he continued, just in case I didn't hear him the first time.

The elevator doors opened, and I stepped inside. "Wow, maybe this is the first time we've ever agreed on something."

He swiped his card and pressed the buttons for both my floor then his.

We rode the first level in silence, ascending with a thickness in the air. I looked over at Ari, and his eyes were glued to me, heat and energy in them I couldn't ignore.

"Ari, you can't look at me like that after what we just agreed."

He stepped so close the lapels on his suit jacket touched my blouse. His scent of manly sandalwood was intoxicating and sent me to dirty places. He towered over me, pulling me into him, then his hand circled the nape of my neck and tipped my face up to his.

My heart pounded in my chest. We were at work. At any moment, the elevator doors could fly open. But my hands fell around his muscular arms, finding their way to the curves of his biceps.

"I want to fuck you in this elevator," he groaned out in a husky voice that sent my knees to jelly.

His eyes burned dark, half-hooded. They dragged to my lips, and I parted in response. I tilted my head up, love drunk on his hypnotic eyes, and I whispered, "Why do you chase me? You don't like me, Ari." I ran my hands up and down his arms.

"Don't like you?" He threaded his fingers through a loose strand of my hair, gliding it over the curve of my ear. "I adore you, Olivia, and it scares the living shit out of me."

I sucked in a breath, blinking while trying to comprehend his words.

What? No.

This was too fast, too crazy, and not at all who Ari Goldsmith was. He was an arrogant, full-of-himself playboy. Not this sensitive, gorgeous man whose vulnerability had sideswiped me and cleared the air from my lungs.

The elevator slowed, and I stepped back from him and his honey words. "Well, if it scares the shit out of you, listen to your gut because it never lies."

He squeezed his eyes shut, and when he opened them, he let out a forceful breath. The elevator doors opened and standing in the hallway stood Ari's assistant, Vivienne.

She looked from me to Ari. My mouth ran dry, and my stomach tightened.

"Ari, Olivia, welcome back." She stepped inside but still, I couldn't move.

"This is your floor, Ms. Willows," Ari asserted. "Careful the door doesn't hit you on the way out."

Color rose to my cheeks, and I knew the darkness in his tone was all my doing.

Quickly, I walked out of the elevator, then turned back. Ari's beaded eyes stared back at me. Then he was gone.

* * *

Exhaustion eclipsed the work I was doing, and when I looked outside, it was night. The sky was black, and the moon's glow fanned through the ornate art deco windows and into my office.

I checked my phone. It was after eight. No wonder my stomach was rumbling. Three missed calls from Lourde and various texts on our group chat flashed up. How had I missed sixty-one messages, and what was so important that Pepper, Lourde, and Evelyn needed to talk that much?

Curious, I opened the chat, trying to play catchup, and jumped in midway down the trail of messages.

Lourde: *So girls, I can't reach Olivia and wanted to tell you all together sooo…*

Evelyn: *So?*

Evelyn: *Don't leave me hanging…*

Pepper: *Don't leave us both hanging…*

Lourde: *So, pack your bags and cancel your plans for this weekend because Vegas is calling, and we are leaving Friday night!*

Pepper: *Hell yes! Is this what Connor was holding back from telling me?*

Evelyn: *As in tomorrow? And why Vegas?*

Pepper: *Wait, are the hunkholes coming?*

Lourde: *Everyone's coming! Connor and Barrett organized it all and just told me.*

Pepper: *Yuss!! Heels, dresses, and drinks.*

Lourde: And don't forget baccarat and blackjack.
Evelyn: *I don't think I can come.*
Lourde: *Barrett thought you might say that, so he has rearranged all your physio appointments and organized a helicopter to pick you up and meet us at the Airport.*
Evelyn: *Are you kidding me? That's excessive.*
Lourde: *That's who he is.*
Pepper: *That's who they both are. Connor has organized the Diamond Jet to take us there, so we are traveling in style.*
Lourde: *Only the best!*
Evelyn: *What is this all for?*
Pepper: *Do we need a reason to go to Vegas?*
Evelyn: *I've never been.*
Pepper: *OMG, we will show you the ropes, hun. After a few margaritas, you will love life.*
Lourde: *I cannot wait… now, where is Olivia!*

Vegas. With Ari. Um, okay. I set my phone on my desk and stared at it, hoping the answer would come to me.

If I said no, I knew Pepper and Lourde wouldn't have any of it. And if I went, what would happen with Ari?

From our last exchange on the elevator, I didn't know where we stood. Whether or not he hated me, if we were back to that, and from his stare in the elevator, I sure pissed him off, but it was for the best. He adored me, but it scared the hell out of him. *Why?* I shook my head. It didn't matter why because I didn't have time for a relationship, not when my family depended on me and not when I relied on myself to get ahead in life.

But I was entitled to a good time away with my girlfriends. I could hide whatever was going on between Ari and me, and he sure as hell could do the same.

I picked up my phone and thumbed out a quick reply.

Olivia: *"I'm in,"* I said audibly, and a smile peeled on my cheeks.

Three bubbles appeared immediately.

Lourde: *A M A Z I N G! 6:00 p.m. sharp at Teterboro Airport.*

"You're still here?" An emphysema-laced voice sounded, and I immediately knew who it was. Instantly, I looked up and swallowed.

"Mr. Sanella, hello," I said, keeping it formal and regarded the man led by his overhanging belly enter my office.

I recoiled. Something about the man gave me the creeps, and with only me remaining on my floor, I thought it prudent to leave. I stood and closed my laptop. "I was just leaving." Grabbing my phone, I slid it into the side pocket of my briefcase, then pushed my chair underneath the desk.

"How was your trip?" he asked, unmoving and ignoring every social cue I hinted at.

"Great." I followed up with another response, "Productive."

"I can't wait to see how it all turns out. I hope Ari's showing you the ropes and taking care of you."

"Yes, I'm in good hands," I said, walking around my desk and realizing how that might have sounded.

"I'm sure you are." He choked out a laugh. When I looked up, his gaze hit mine, and a smugness hid behind his wrinkled gray eyes. His response hung in the air like an uncomfortable insinuation. Everything I'd ever worked for could be gone in an instant, and I immediately tangled with rage. He had crossed a professional boundary, and I didn't care who he was.

"Is there something you want to say, Mr. Sanella?"

I was fully aware of the harassment rumors that surrounded William Sanella. His treatment of women was known all too well in the tight-knit industry, and even over lunch this week, I overheard a girl on my team make comments about his abrupt forwardness toward them.

"You are a feisty one, aren't you?"

I narrowed my eyes. Frustrated, I pulled my bag closer, gripping it between my fingers.

"Not at all," I replied, throwing him a large fake smile.

He let out a laugh from the depths of his bulging belly. And my skin crawled.

Get out, Olivia, before you let your temper take over and ruin everything you've worked so hard to create.

"I have to go, have a good night, Mr. Sanella." Quickly, I walked round my desk and out of my office, not looking back when he called my name.

I needed a break to let loose.

Vegas, here we come…

14

ARI

Between pouring over accounting documents and employing a forensic officer to hunt for the missing millions, Friday came in a flash, which was good because Vegas called my name, and I was so keen for this trip.

I teetered back and forth with my feelings for Olivia. It didn't help that she pushed me away every chance she got, especially when I cared a lot about her. But I needed to let loose and clear my head. Vegas was just the medicine I needed.

"Cheers to a fun weekend," Connor said, holding up his glass of whiskey as the plane slingshot into the air. We all held up our glasses, and I swallowed down the liquid amber, relaxation not hitting the mark like it normally would.

Olivia's quick change from business attire to party girl had me doing a double-take. She must have changed at the office because there's no way she would have had time to go home, then double back to the airport.

Gorgeous and intelligent, she stirred something within me. Something that had been lying dormant for a decade, something I tried to ignore for fear of being hurt again. Dressed in a royal-blue dress that accentuated her eyes and a plunging neckline, it took every ounce of strength inside me to stop staring. Not that it stopped Magnus. No, I had to elbow him a few times during the plane ride so his eyes set on something else, anything but her.

We'd ignored each other on the five-hour journey into Vegas, which was probably a good thing because I sure as hell didn't want to hear the girls go back and forth about Lourde's wedding plans. I was highly confident they weren't interested in the sordid details of Magnus' latest threesome he shared so freely with Connor, Barrett, and me.

* * *

After we'd checked into the Bellagio, we headed down to the hotel's club lounge. With the time difference and the flight time, it was past midnight by the time we wedged around the seating and hit the dance floor. Still early in Vegas time with the night just kicking off.

I watched her dance on the floor packed with hundreds of people. She was easy to spot for me. Blue dress with striking short blonde hair, she danced like no one was watching, and I had this overwhelming desire to take her in my arms and slow dance with her.

But here, with the guys, I couldn't risk it. I didn't want to, she was a beauty, but anything more than a fling was too much for me.

Then why did it sting like a pack of European wasps when she pushed you away in the elevator?

And why did I want nothing more than to be with her, pry her open, peel her layers back like an onion, and take care of her? Because, like me, she was guarded, and I wanted to know why. I wanted to protect her and show her I could handle her. All of her—every curve of her hips, every snarky remark, and every roadblock she hurled in my direction.

Without losing sight of her, I got up, leaving Evelyn, Lourde, and Barrett at the table together with Magnus. Connor and Pepper had disappeared off the dance floor and now was my opportunity.

I shouldered my way through the crowd, making my way toward her as she swayed to her own beat. But as I neared, a guy cinched his way around her waist. She kept dancing and did not swat his hand away. Instead, she tipped her head back as he nudged closer, enjoying the guy's company.

What the actual fuck?

A fling.

That's all I was.

She turned to face the man, and I was now only a few feet behind them both. She danced with him, and fuck, it stung. Her hips glided to the beat, her body moving seductively. Was she drunk? How much had she had to drink? Every time I saw her, she had a drink in her hands.

A woman with a hot-pink sash approached me, and I let her. Gorgeous, she and her friends hovered beside me. One of her friends leaned in.

"It's my friend's bachelorette night. Want to show her a good time?" She purred.

"Sure," I said as I wrapped my hands around her friend's little curves.

"Why are you getting married?" I asked her while she ground against me in a dress that left little to the imagination.

She laughed. "What kind of question is that?"

I shrugged as she held onto my arms, a smile playing seductively on her lips.

"I love him, that's why."

"I see."

"But that doesn't mean we can't have some fun," she said, pushing her body up to mine, her breasts pressing into my chest.

"Is that so?" I questioned, but my eyes drifted to Olivia. Except she wasn't there anymore.

I pulled away from the girl in my arms and frantically looked around the room for Olivia. Fuck, she better not have left with him. The thought made my body build with rage.

Thank fuck I was tall because I scanned the room with ease, but still, she was nowhere to be found.

"Hey. You okay?" I looked down momentarily at the woman in my arms.

"Best of luck with your wedding," I said, removing my hands and kissing her on the cheek.

"Seriously?" she protested, but by then, I was walking away from the dance floor toward the front doors, where I swear for a second I saw her.

"Move," I said, pushing people out the way so I could not lose sight of her. Then, when the crowd had cleared, I spotted her. Glaring.

She was by herself. Relief flooded my body, but then I took her in. Ramrod straight, a scowl stretched across her features.

"Where are you going?" I asked when I caught up with her.

"Back to my room."

"Alone?"

"Alone, Ari."

"Good, because I don't know what I would have done if you had left with that cocksucker who had his hands around your waist." Her eyes widened. "Yes, I saw you and him, and it took every ounce of strength not to break you apart and smash his nose in with my fist."

She folded her arms. "You ought to talk. That girl was half your age."

"No... don't even," I said, holding my hand up.

"You can't be serious," she yelled. "So you can, but I can't, is that it?"

"You said we were a fling, Olivia… and for your information, I was on my way to wrap my hands around your body when said dickhead beat me to it."

"So what, you just gave up when you saw someone else?" *Was she mocking me? Did she not think I had the balls to match that dick with his hands on her waist?* "Yeah, that's it, then you shack up with someone half your age, out of spite? Is that it?"

"Don't fucking play with me, Olivia. I don't like games," I warned.

She shook her head and turned abruptly, heading for the exit in her stilettos.

My skin flushed with rage as confusion swept over me. She wanted me. Everything about her said so except her damn words.

I followed her, close behind, as I practically ran out of the club.

She turned when she reached the hotel elevators. "Leave me alone, Ari," she said, banging the call button with her fist.

My chest rose and fell with pent-up anger and frustration. This woman, what was she doing to me? Whatever I did, I couldn't stay away, and fuck, I didn't want to stay away anymore.

The doors opened, and she immediately went inside, swiping the card to her floor and leaving me standing as she slunk into the corner. I quickly jumped in before the elevator doors closed, banging my shoulder into the metal door as it closed on me. I stepped into the other corner opposite her. The space between us grew thick with the familiar feeling of anger and desire.

The elevator jerked north, and suddenly, I stepped forward, banging my fist on the red stop button. The high-pitched alarm sounded, bringing it to a jarring halt.

"What do you think you're doing?" She shrieked as she

held onto the rail behind her, fear behind her eyes. But it wasn't me she feared. It was us.

I stepped in toward her recognizing that same fear within me, but I no longer had control over it or my own emotions.

"Olivia, stop fighting this." I gazed into her blue eyes and tilted her head toward me. She looked up at me. A vulnerability flashed for a millisecond before disappearing altogether.

"I can't, Ari," she whispered in a strain.

I took her chin with both hands feeling her tremble with my touch. Inhaling her scent, my dick stood at attention, wanting to claim every inch of her body. My lips brushed hers, gently then with more vigor. Olivia arched her back as my hands fell around her hips, trailing kisses down the line of her neck. She let out a sigh, and fuck, that damn sound sent my pulse to the stratosphere.

I pulled back, my length still pushing against her dress. Her eyes were dark and full of wanting and desire. The same that mirrored mine.

I dropped my head to hers, and our foreheads touched. Gazing into her ocean-blues, I said, "Tell me you don't want me. Tell me you don't want my hands on your body, and I promise to never touch you again."

She opened her mouth to speak, but nothing came out. With her back against the wall, she sucked in a breath, and I waited, a twisting feeling pooling in the pit of my stomach as every second ticked by. I feared a rejection was waiting to happen.

15

OLIVIA

My heart beat erratically. It had since he chased me out of the club and followed me into the elevator. Goddamn, I hoped there was a defibrillator nearby because, at any moment, my heart would tear open.

Ari's head lowered to my forehead, and warmth replaced the cool of my skin. His eyes, dangerous and vulnerable at the same time, spoke to me like no other man had before.

"Tell me you don't want me. Tell me you don't want my hands on your body, and I promise to never touch you again."

Oh fuck. Fuckity fuck. I want your hands all over my body like a nasty rash.

I didn't understand it.

I just knew I needed him.

I stared into his eyes as his look changed from a question to concern with my lack of response. Goddamn, girl, think with your heart for just one moment.

I put my hand up to his jaw and pulled him down to me so his eyes were level with mine. "I don't think I can tell you that," I whispered in a hoarse voice.

A smile peeled onto his mouth. "Thank fuck," he said, and his lips crashed onto mine. He tasted of whiskey and anticipation and shit. Were my knees going weak at the connection?

I pulled back, desire pooling in my core like it always did with this man around. "Here?" I asked.

"As much as I want to fuck you in this elevator, I will wait to take you back to my penthouse, where I can devour you on every surface imaginable."

He turned, pulled the card out of his jacket, and swiped it, hitting the top floor. With a jerk, the elevator resumed its original ascension.

Then his lips were on mine again. I pulled him close, all inhibition going out the window as Ari was the only thing on my mind.

Luckily, the elevator door opened because I wouldn't last much longer, especially when his fingers made their way up and under my dress. Pushing the fabric of my lace thong aside, he massaged my aching clit with his long, strong fingers.

After he opened the door, he pulled me inside and turned to me.

"I want to take you to the bedroom first. Then we have all night to explore the other surfaces in this shiny penthouse."

"I like the sound of that."

"Now get over here before my dick tears a hole in my pants."

Swinging my hips overtly, I walked seductively to him, unable to wait another moment for his hands to trespass my body.

"Fuck me, you are something else." With one move, he lifted me, folding me over his shoulder as he kicked off his shoes and walked through the penthouse.

Neon lights from the strip below lit up the penthouse just enough to make out the living room he was walking through and heading to the bedroom.

He slapped my ass hard, and I dug my nails into his broad shoulders from the force.

He groaned in response. "I ought to spank you harder for what you're doing to me, Ms. Willows." Then he did it again, harder.

I let out a yelp, my breath hitching in my throat from the sting that remained. He rubbed his hand over the cheek, and my sex clenched at his touch and the burning heat that lingered.

"What is it I'm d-doing t-to you, Ari?" I stuttered out.

"Fuck knows. But I can't seem to get enough of you."

I closed my eyes in a calming breath, his damn words making me nervous.

He pushed open the bedroom door with his shoulder, then slid me down off his shoulder and to the front of his chest. My dress climbed up my thighs as my heels landed on the polished floor.

"Well, let's enjoy tonight then," I said, dragging my hand through my bob, then placing my hands on his chest. I fanned my fingers out and pressed their pads against his wall of muscles, dragging them down the contours of his stomach. His eyes darted down, half hooded and dark, and his chest rose and fell with anticipation.

He ached for me as much as I did him, and it turned me on more than I liked to admit.

"Enjoy?" His hands rounded my bottom. Then his thumbs slid between my hip bones and my lace thong, making me moist with anticipation. "Ms. Willows, I plan to sink myself into you slowly, then watch you beg me to stop."

I sucked in my lower lip. Fuck. This dirty talk was on another level, and an undeniable feverish ache overtook my body.

"What if I want it fast, not slow?" I hissed out, unsure I could survive his slow assault. His mouth sunk onto the exposed part of my neck, and I tilted to the side, giving him free rein to ravish my body.

Immediately, he pulled down my dress and thong so they pooled around my ankles. As he ravaged my neck, most likely leaving marks—which I couldn't care less about—I kicked off my clothing and pushed up against him. Seeking friction, I rubbed my clit against the fabric of his pants and the thickness that lay erect underneath.

"That's it, sugar. Rub yourself on me, hard and fast."

And so I did. I lost any inhibitions and rubbed my sensitive button on him, panting in desire. He lifted me so I was level with his waist, and I wrapped my legs around his body. Pushing me against the wall, he held me, pinning me upright with the weight of his body. His dick rubbed against my sweet spot as I gyrated harder against him. I groaned in arousal, and his mouth didn't stop. Connecting with my neck, he trailed a line of kisses down, grazing my nipples. His touch sent me into overdrive.

"You are all mine, Olivia." Ari peered up, then flicked my nipple with his tongue before taking it between his teeth and biting just hard enough to tip me over the edge of no return.

"Fuck, Ari." I shuddered around him, my body playing hostage to his touch.

When I looked down, his mouth still toyed around my breast, a smirk playing on his lips. Damn, it was the hottest thing.

"I just came rubbing myself on you." I burst out laughing and thought that's something you did in grade school rather than with a guy in his thirties.

"And now you're going to come with my dick in your sweet tight pussy."

"So presumptuous." I smiled, and his grip around me grew stronger before his mouth took mine for a hot, wet kiss. He groaned in my mouth, and the sound made me hot again, wanting him all over.

He put me down and, in one quick move, lowered his pants and unbuttoned his shirt. Ripples of muscles led to his carved torso, and like a marble Greek god, he stood with the ambient light highlighting his chiseled chest.

"Very," he said, taking his dick in his hands and stroking the full eight inches from base to tip. Ready and wanting me, his dark eyes drank me in. I wanted him like vampires wanted blood. I stepped closer running my fingers down his golden abs to the dark hairs of his groin, then closing my hands around his and his engorgement.

He hissed out at the connection.

"Painfully slow?" I questioned, echoing his previous sentiment.

He groaned out, "Yes, I want to savor every bit of you."

"Like this?" I slid one hand between my thighs and sunk a finger inside my pussy. Removing it, I dragged my cum along the seam of his dick, making it slick with moisture.

His eyes widened, and I glided my hand back and forth around his erection.

"Fuck me, Ms. Willows, you are going to break me."

"Lie down," he ordered, and without hesitation, I released him and walked over to the bed. I lay on my back and watched him wrap himself, contemplating how he would feel inside me naked and without protection. Quickly, I struck the thought from my mind.

He climbed on top of me, stopping to spread my legs apart. Then he paused, nipping at my apex. Trailing the inside of my thigh, he peppered me with gentle kisses that sent my pulse racing and skin flush with arousal.

"I can't get enough of you." He peered up, his pupils appearing larger as he maintained steady eye contact.

"Then don't stop," I said breathlessly, his stare making me wanton and needy for only him.

Inhaling deeply, he tilted his head, and with his eyes bonded to mine, his tongue lashed across my clit at the same time his fingers filled me. I groaned out, fluttering my eyes closed and breaking eye contact. My back arched off the bed as uncontrollable flushes of heat spread across my stomach.

Filling me further, I moaned, unable to keep my voice quiet, my hands tugging at the roots of his hair.

Slow. Painfully slow, I was building again, and true to Ari's word, he ate me out slowly. When I was almost combusting, he drew back.

"Ari, please," I pleaded in a gravelly voice I didn't recognize.

"Tell me what you need, Olivia."

"I need you, Ari. Now."

He rounded to his knees and lowered himself onto me, his thickness finding exactly where he belonged. Ari inched in slowly, and I clenched around his head.

"Relax for me," he said, his tone provoking me to find his eyes as he stood on his haunches over me.

As soon as I stared into his big dark browns, my body was at his command, and he inched further inside me until he was all the way in. He started a steady rhythm, slow and sensual, his hips grinding back and forth. This was the missionary position on steroids, and fuck, I needed air.

I squeezed my eyes shut as my body built higher. "Open your eyes. I want you to look at me when you come, princess."

Never wanting this connection to end, I obeyed his words. Then I pulled my arms around him, my nails clawing down his back and holding his firm ass.

He groaned. "Olivia, come for me," he demanded, and after another deep thrust, he stretched me completely, my body tensing then unfurling around him in an explosive orgasm.

Intensity gripped, and with his eyes seeing into my soul, there was an intimacy between us I couldn't explain. A moment later, he groaned a throaty, deep guttural groan as his eyes remained on mine, and he released into me.

Intensity floored me, never had I kept eye contact with a man while he was coming. *Had he ever done that with another woman? He is staring at you, do not go there, Olivia.*

Instead of letting interrogative thoughts take over, which was my go-to with Ari, I leaned up and kissed him. Warm and breathy, his tongue massaged mine in a seductive kiss that made the hairs on my neck stand up at attention.

"Well…" he said and got up to disappear into the bathroom to clean up. When he returned, he ran a hand through his hair, and goddamn, he looked scorching adorable.

"Well?" I replied.

"Can I get you a glass of wine?"

I felt a pang of disappointment arrow through me. Furrowing my brow, I wanted him to commit to his earlier deal.

"What is it?" he asked as he walked over to the bed, coming to sit beside me.

"What makes you think there's something?" I asked, fidgeting with both my thumbs in my lap. *Blushing and fidgeting now too?* Strange.

"Olivia. I want you. You want me. We have to be honest with each other."

"Okay," I said, picking up an invisible piece of lint from the duvet. "All I was going to say was, we haven't explored the kitchen surfaces yet."

He leaned in and kissed me, then stepped back with a smirk forming along his jaw. "Or the shower…" His eyes went dark and beady, that look I was so familiar with, doing things to my lady parts like nobody's business.

"Or the shower," I echoed.

He took his hand up to my face and stroked my cheek with his thumb. An unexplainable warmth flooded my body, and there was nowhere else I wanted to be than with Ari Goldsmith.

16

ARI

The scent of fruity sweetness woke me. Her breasts nuzzled against my ribcage, short blonde hair splayed across my chest, and a velvety smooth arm draped precariously close to my morning glory. Damn, how my dick had the energy to salute the sun blew me.

After what we did last night and into the morning, I don't know how the stallion had anything left in the tank.

Yes, every surface.

Housekeeping had a definite task ahead of them.

Casting my gaze down, I felt the warmth of her breath on my skin. She drew and released deep, quiet breaths, her body stone-still, featherlight against my side. Now, this was a view I could certainly get used to.

Contrasting wholly to the debating Ice Queen, this woman was something else. But if she thought she could push me away, she thought wrong. I couldn't get enough, nor would I stay the fuck away. And neither would she.

The attraction was undeniable. Then if pure attraction wasn't enough, there was that lingering feeling.

A feeling that was familiar a decade ago when I was dating Sophia.

A feeling I never thought I'd have again.

Until now.

Carefully, I ran my hand down her hair, moving it off her face. She moaned and adjusted slightly but did not wake. Her cheeks glowed pink, and her lips were swollen from the endless kissing. Damn, I followed the line of her jaw down to her neck, where I punished her with bruising kisses, leaving a hailstone of blue and pink bruises where my mouth had been all night long.

Fuck. Would she be pissed off? I wasn't sure. Her moods could flip like a coin toss.

The truth was, I didn't know too much about Olivia, but I was determined to find out more today.

Gently, I slid out from under her, and she flopped down, her head sliding off the pillow. I smiled at the sight of her, sheet half splayed down her body, revealing her slender sun-kissed back and dead asleep.

My stomach knotted as emotion clogged my throat. I quickly grabbed my sweat pants from my nearby wardrobe and legged into them. Glancing back, I pulled the sheet up to around her bare shoulders, then, with one last glance, I walked out of the bedroom and into the kitchen.

Deciding work emails were never going away, I opened my laptop and started replying to them one at a time. I was so close to finding out where the anomaly was with Grandmama's missing millions but still so far.

When I thought I had come close, the trail went cold. Twice that had happened, and twice I went with my tail between my legs, having to report the news to Grandmama.

Patient and kind, she said to keep going. We had no other option but to keep going. So when an email came through from the forensic accounting team I'd hired, I quickly clicked on it.

Aristotle,

You are right in suggesting we dig further into the July files. Things are definitely not as they seem, and the subsidiary account shows a different amount to the bank transactions. The next step is to trace the pool of over one hundred bank accounts with nominal amounts.

The first payment came in July, and subsequent payments have been spread across the last four years. It will take time, but rest assured, we have the best forensic team for the job.

Sincerely,

Callum Grulder
President
Forensic Accounting Incorporated

I pushed my laptop away. I fucking knew it. And now I was so close to proving it. Not only did I think it was an inside job, but whoever was behind it was cunning and intelligent, spreading payments over multiple accounts and dates, making my job even harder.

Immediately, I reached for my phone and called Grandmama, elated to share some good news.

"Aristotle," she said, half coughing as she answered the phone.

"Grandmama, are you all right?" I asked, concerned as her cough sounded deep and chesty. She'd had pneumonia before, and it took her two weeks in the hospital to recover.

"Fine, fine. How's Vegas?"

"Like Vegas always is, wild and liberating."

"Ah, I remember." She laughed.

Stories of Farrah Goldsmith's wild child days were epic. A

fashion house, and once a model herself, she partied with the best of them.

"Is everything on track for the opening next week?"

"Yes, perfectly fine. We will be back on Monday and head straight into the store to meet the cabinet fitters."

"Is Olivia with you in Vegas?"

Shit. Olivia would kill me if Farrah knew we were sleeping together.

"Yes, we're all here. Barrett, Lourde, Pepper and Connor, Magnus, and Evelyn, Barrett's sister."

"I see," she said, remaining silent and waiting for me to reply. "So much for hating her then, Aristotle?"

"Put it this way. She's grown on me."

"I like her," she said, a smile sounding down the line. And damn, my grandmama was like a wolf on a scent. Picking up on trails is what she did best. All my life, she'd been that way.

"Well, you hired her," I retorted. "The reason for my call was that we are onto something with the accounting issue."

"Oh?" She sounded surprised.

"The company I hired has reiterated what I found in the July files."

"And?"

"And whoever is behind this is a smart son of a bitch, so it will take some time, but we will get him or her."

"Excellent. My decades of sweat aren't for anyone to fuck with but me."

I raised a surprised brow. My Grandmama never swore. "No, it's not. I'll get them."

"Hey!" Olivia chorused jubilantly as she appeared in the doorframe with the sheet wrapped around her body. As soon as she realized I was on the phone, she covered her mouth before quickly lowering them to mouth the word, "Sorry."

I covered the phone receiver at the same time Grandmama spoke.

"Well, you certainly sound like you have your hands full. Enjoy Vegas."

"Thanks, Grandmama." The line went dead, and my gaze dragged up the slit in the sheet, revealing her caramel thigh. A shocked look morphed onto her naturally made-up face.

"That was Farrah?" She gasped, taking her hands to her mouth.

I nodded.

"Oh my God!" She paced the length of the room, then stopped. "Do you think she heard me? What if… oh God." Her hand lifted to her forehead, and she rubbed the sides of her temples, clearly in distress.

I watched her go from sleepy to completely freaked out. And this time, I wasn't the cause.

"Calm down." I closed my laptop and hurried to where she pounded the tiles with her bare feet.

"I can't calm down. I'm not the type to ever do something like this," she said, her voice tense and laden with anxiety.

"Sleep with the boss?" I said, laughing.

She stopped and stared at me as I approached her. "Exactly, and put my job at risk. This is not funny, Ari."

"Last time I checked, I was your boss, and sugar, your position is perfectly fine." A grin peeled across my cheeks.

I reached out to touch her arm, but she started pacing the floor again.

"This is not good. It's not good." Olivia pulled the sheet around her tightly, her skin flushing red. Sure, I understood it wouldn't be ideal if Farrah had heard, but was it that anxiety-inducing for her? There must be something else at play here.

Calmly and carefully, I walked over to where she stopped and stared out the vast glass windows that opened to a buzzing city below.

"Olivia. What's really going on?" I asked as calmly as

possible for fear of the Ice Queen returning. I kept my distance, purposely not touching her.

She turned, her face screwed up in, what was that, fear?

"I can't lose my job. It's everything to me, Ari, and just when my parents are nearly bailed out."

What? "Your parents are in jail."

"What?" she asked, her mind racing. "No. No, nothing like that."

"I'm not sleeping with the daughter of an axe murderer, am I?"

"Ari, shh," she said, and I was relieved to find a slight smile appear on her flushed skin.

Seizing the opportunity, I took her hand and led her to where I had just been sitting. I sat and pulled her down so she perched on my knee. Thankfully, she didn't pull back when I tugged her closer. "Then tell me. Maybe I can help."

She stared up from her fidgeting fingers, then back down again. Her voice was low and soft when she spoke. "I grew up poor, really poor." Her eyes darted to mine, and I had never seen her look more vulnerable until this moment, so much so that I wanted her to open up to me and peel back more layers.

"Go on… please." I almost begged of her.

"We didn't know where our next meal was coming from, poor."

"Oh." The thought of Olivia as a hungry little girl clawed at my chest.

"We lived in the projects. Welfare wasn't enough to cover our living costs, and Mom was sick. Dad had to take care of me while she underwent treatment for breast cancer. She pulled through, but in an attempt to make ends meet, Dad invested what tiny bit of money we had left into a money-making scheme one of his friends suggested."

"Fuck, nooo…"

She looked up, and her eyes glazed over, wet with unshed tears. My chest squeezed, and I slid my hand from her waist. Then, taking her hands in mine, I intertwined my fingers in hers.

"But, of course, we didn't have enough money to invest in the scheme to make the really big bucks, so they suggested a loan."

I felt sick to my stomach. "Who would lend someone money without the ability to pay it back?"

"Sharks, money-hungry asshole sharks with fancy Manhattan offices, that's who. And charging upward of twenty percent interest. His friend got him onto this deal, but he couldn't blame him. It was the rich." She looked up at me when she said that. "The rich Manhattan sharks who took him for everything, and when I say everything, I mean the man's soul was taken too. They left him a broken man who carried the guilt of his sins."

A familiar pain lashed my chest. The burden of my sins had never left me, either.

I pushed it away.

This wasn't about me.

This was about dear, sweet Olivia.

"The truth is, I've been helping them pay back this debt ever since I started working for Barrett and earning decent money."

She looked up at me, and her honesty took me aback. I brought my hand to her cheek. "I promise you, Olivia, your contract is secure here."

She nodded reassuringly, her lips rolling into her mouth as she ran her tongue over them in relief. "Thank you," she said, keeping her eyes on the floor.

"I'm sorry you had to go through that. It must have been tough."

"It made me tough," she stated with that defiance I initially disliked. But now, I understood this part of her. Things made sense.

"Not all rich people are assholes, though."

"No?" she countered.

"Are you calling me an asshole again?"

She shook her head. "No." She smiled at me before her gaze returned to the floor.

"Please don't assume things about me, Olivia. Ask me, okay?"

"Deal." Her swollen lips twisted into a smile.

My gaze hovered to where the sheet outlined her nipples.

"I know a way you can get a pay raise." A smirk the size of the Grand Canyon appeared on my face.

She laughed, then with a quick rise of her hand, she went to slap me. Anticipating it, I blocked her hand and held it in mine. The sheet she had been holding slid down her chest, pooling around her stomach, her tear-drop breasts on full display and begging for my hand.

She stared at me, a fire burning behind her eyes and something else.

That something else that pulled at my chest.

The same something else I had experienced watching her lie in bed with her head on my chest.

"I need a shower," she said, digging her teeth into her lower lip.

"You do. You're very dirty," I said before adding, "And so am I."

Her smile lit up the room, and before I could add anything, she got up, losing the sheet completely, and made her way into the bathroom.

Like a puppy with a bone, I followed.

* * *

She guided the soapy loofah along the ridges of my shoulders to the nape of my neck. Her nipples elongated, pressing into my back.

Why had I not had anyone wash me before?

"Thank you for listening before," she said.

I lowered my head, the water beading in my hair and down my face. "You know I could pay back your debt, Olivia, but I also know you wouldn't want that."

"You're beginning to know me, Ari." The sponge followed the contours of my back down lower to the indent of my buttocks.

"Perhaps it's because that ice-cold exterior of yours is melting day by day, and you're no longer an Ice Queen."

She turned abruptly so we were face to face, her eyes narrowed to the size of raisins. "Ice Queen?"

"My nickname for you when I wanted a large sinkhole to swallow you up and shut that pretty mouth of yours."

Alarm flickered across her face, then she ran her sponge down the front of my stomach, down each muscle of my chest until she reached my dick. A fire burned behind her eyes as she dropped the sponge and wrapped her hands over my cock. Hard and firm, she tugged it with one hand before cupping my balls with the other.

I was literally in her hands, and it equally terrified and aroused me.

"The feeling was mutual." She smirked.

"Was?" I hissed out on a breath as she stroked me from base to tip, her hurried strokes making me thicker between her grip.

"Was," she echoed before dropping to her knees.

17

OLIVIA

"She won't tell me," Lourde said.

Tucked in the private room, we all sat around the oval table in Vegas' newest and hottest Italian restaurant, Nero. Everything was black—black walls, black plates, black cutlery, and black linens. The chef's idea was to not detract from the food itself with fancy decor but to let the food shine against a black backdrop. It was an experience in itself.

Overhead hung a massive chandelier, black, of course, and the only color in the room was the ambient warmth of the yellow glow from the light that shone on the table.

"Has anyone else got a motherfucking hangover like me?" Magnus volunteered, swallowing down his dish of squid ink tagliolini.

"No, I don't need to drink to excess to have fun," Evelyn said. "We aren't in our twenties anymore."

Magnus' brows lifted into his forehead. "Sorry, Ms. Trunchbull!"

"Yeah, but we are in Vegas, sis," Barrett said. "What happens in Vegas..."

"Stays in Vegas," I finished his sentence, and the gaze of

the table fell upon me. Even in the dimly lit room, I felt his stare. Then his foot, from underneath the table, nudged mine.

We agreed to keep this quiet. Whatever this was, I wasn't entirely sure, but Ari was not who I thought he was. Did that mean we'd see each other beyond the opening of the store? Hope bubbled inside my chest.

"Did you want to add something, Olivia? Like where you disappeared to last night at the nightclub?" Pepper asked, tilting her head, a smile on her mouth.

"Or, why you are wearing a scarf in the desert?" Barrett added.

My heart went *boom boom boom*, and I avoided Ari's stares like a magnet that had lost its magnetism.

"Since when have you asked about my dress sense?" I countered to Barrett. In the years I'd worked at his company, never once had he said a word.

"Who was he?" Ari asked, finally contributing to the conversation.

Cue to stare at him point blank, I spoke up, "A lady never tells."

The table erupted into laughter. "Even to me?" Lourde pried beside me, whispering as she leaned in.

"Honestly, I didn't catch his name," I said, feigning an embarrassed look on my face.

"God, she's the female version of the hunkholes," Pepper quipped, clapping her hands together in delight.

"No, she's not!" Lourde protested.

"Okay, maybe half the hunkholes then," Connor said. He looked at Barrett, then raised his glass. "We've met our soulmates."

"Oh God," Magnus said. "Can we hit the club already?"

"No, I want dessert!" Evelyn expressed.

"Of course you do." Magnus deadpanned.

"You can wait a little longer for some West Coast pussy," Evelyn pointed out aloud, and suddenly, the table went quiet.

Heads turned like lasers, not believing what we had just heard. Evelyn was the mature one in the group, and I had never heard her swear before, let alone use the word pussy, until now.

"Will the real Eve please stand up," Pepper said, pumping her hands into the air, then giving her a high five.

The waiter came and took away our plates. Throughout dinner, Ari's leg rubbed against mine, and with it being dark, he got away with it.

When dessert came around, we devoured the Amaretti and raisin cheesecake like a seagull to leftover chips.

Meanwhile, I ignored the conversation down the other end of the table, where Pepper, Connor, Magnus, and Evelyn debated the credentials of the new Knicks' coach. Sports... *ugh*. Tune out time. Instead, I took to savoring my last mouthful of dessert.

"This really is an orgasm on a plate," I said, licking my lips. "Who is the chef?"

"Francesco Gallo," Barrett said. "He worked in Sicily for years under world-renowned chef, Petro Donati, and has since ventured out on his own. This is his first restaurant, and if I'm not mistaken, I hear the waitlist is over a year."

"Well, it's so damn good," Lourde said, eating hers and polishing off Barrett's desert too.

"Did you say a year? How on earth did we get in then?"

Barrett looked over at Ari, and I shifted my gaze to him. "You're staring at him. Chefs, models, celebrities... Ari knows them all."

Instantly, my heart did something weird, my stomach sunk a little lower, and I knew it wasn't from the food. Was that jealousy? Since when...

"I bet he does," I commented, and Ari stared at me. A curiosity lingered behind his brown eyes.

Conversations stopped around us as Ari and I collided in our gaze.

"Jealous?" he countered as he lifted his whiskey to his lips, taking a large swig. Putting the glass down, a smirk played on his glistening lips.

"Of you? P... lease."

"And here I was thinking you guys were getting along," Lourde added.

"I know. I was thinking the same," Barrett added.

"Who, with the Ice Queen?" Ari added. And I knew it was a show to keep up the charade, but it still stung a little.

Sensing my discomfort, his leg extended underneath the table connected with mine. I pulled away abruptly. Glancing around the table, I didn't think anyone had noticed, but damn, I had to be more careful.

"What is it with you two?" Barrett looked between Ari and me.

"Ask the Ice Queen. She is as flippant as the sun during winter."

Why was he taunting me? And did someone shut the damn air off? It was stifling in here. Not one to take anything lying down, I straightened and bit back.

"And he's an arrogant jerk."

"Fierce words," he mocked, getting my back up even more. "From a woman whose work is seriously over-rated."

Lourde, Barrett, and now Pepper and Connor turned in our direction.

"*Ari!*" Lourde shrieked out in my defense. But I could take care of myself. Always have.

I ran a finger between my scarf and neck, loosening the fabric that felt tighter than a boa constrictor around my neck. Ari's eyes shone with mischief, the same look he had when we loathed each other. He had gone for the jugular with that comment, and he knew it would sting.

Well, two could play that game. "Flippant? Me? I think you're mistaking me for yourself. Perhaps that's why what was her name that left you... because you don't have a heart to care about anyone but yourself."

He slammed his glass down, and it was as though a light had been switched on inside him.

His stare put me on a knife's edge.

"Hey, guys, come on," Barrett cautioned.

Fuck, I felt like I was going to die of suffocation.

Lourde leaned in close, "Hey, what's going on?"

"Nothing!" I bit out, wrestling with my scarf. I slid it down my neck, bunching it up in my hand, then flung it over the back of my seat. The feeling of cool air on my skin steadied my frayed nerves.

"Holy fuck is that?" Connor hopped up and walked toward me. By the time I realized what he was looking at, it was too late. "Hickeys! Someone had fun last night!" Connor laughed, setting off cheers and gasps from around the table.

Instantly, I snatched the scarf and wrapped it around my neck, covering it up. But it was too little too late.

A quick glance toward Ari showed his rage was still there but lessened somewhat after sensing my embarrassment. *Did he care? Did he have a heart?*

"Let me see!" Lourde said, peeling away my hand. Pepper rose from her chair to get a closer look. And suddenly, I was center stage. Embarrassment clawed at me, and I blushed from head to toe.

"Who did this to you?" Evelyn said, a huge smile on her lips. "And where can I find him?"

"*Sis!*" Barrett blurted in shock. But any momentary distraction was lost, and all eyes were on me, waiting for an answer.

"I told you, I don't know his name," I whispered, taking a

huge gulp of my Peach Bellini. The sweetness slid down like a dream and briefly pulled me away from this nightmare.

Oh God, where's that sinkhole? I needed one to swallow me whole right this second.

"Just leave her be," Evelyn said to everyone pining over for a closer look.

"I'm fine. I had a great night. But we both got what we wanted from one another. You know?"

"Oh honey, you need to find that man again tonight."

"Or someone else," I countered. Wanting to infuriate Ari like he had me was probably the only thing that made sense to me at the minute because, by now, these games we were playing were too high school. I didn't know where we began and the games finished. The lines were blurred, and so was I.

I felt his bullets from across the room. Was he angry with me, or did he not want me with someone else? Which one was it?

"I'm available!" Magnus piped up, and Barrett and Connor let out a laugh.

"You're always available."

"Exactly."

Knowing that a flat-out no would please Ari, I shrugged, leaving his question unanswered.

"Well, hello," Pepper said.

Ari remained silent, but inside I could tell he was a bubbling furnace waiting to erupt at any moment.

"Let's get the check. I'm ready to party," Magnus stated, a smile on his lips as he stared my way.

Oh fuck stick.

18

ARI

Never had I wanted to reach over the table and slap Magnus more than at that moment he hit on Olivia. And she had encouraged it too. As we walked from the restaurant to the club, with each step, my veins flushed with pent-up rage. I watched Magnus pull closer to her, and it took all my willpower not to take the guy outside and punch his lights out.

She wasn't interested.

I knew that.

We had something. Whether it was a stabbing desire to kill each other or a burning need to have one another, we were inseparable.

This game of hating one another was pleasant enough until it wasn't. Until things got personal. She triggered me again, knowing which buttons to push, knowing exactly how to get my back up. And I played into her hands, into her insecurity. An insecurity I hadn't realized until now when she showed her jealousy at Barrett's remark.

Sure I knew most models, celebrities, and chefs and could

pull a last-minute table at a hatted restaurant, but that was just from living and breathing fashion most of my life. It meant nothing to me, but now, after what we'd been through together, I wondered if she was jealous of these connections, especially of the women in my life. I saw it in her eyes. A second of that vulnerability, and I knew she had to be jealous. More importantly, that meant she knew we were more than just some meaningless fling.

But then she turned that caring into fear and lashed back at me, labeling me a womanizer. That was one thing, but then to say I didn't care for anyone but myself.

Fuck.

If she only knew. If she only knew the depths of emotion I was capable of feeling until I shut that part of me off. Until I buried it so deep inside me, I didn't know if I could feel it again.

Until her.

Everything came to the surface after she stirred that gaping hole inside me.

None of it made sense, nothing at all. Olivia was like no other woman I'd ever been with, but as I watched her swish her hips in the coral pink off-the-shoulder dress, I wasn't sure what to think anymore.

I was in no man's land and needed to speak my mind.

* * *

I couldn't drink.

I needed to be clearheaded.

And it appeared she'd stopped drinking too after dinner.

Instead, she was listening to Magnus talk about his family's IT company—one of the biggest tech companies in America. Still, I read her face like a mirror and could tell he wasn't holding her interest because each time she reached for her soda, she peered up at me through her lashes.

After a while, she slid out from the booth, making her way to the bathroom but not before looking over her shoulder in my direction.

Was that an invitation?

I left the table and stood. "Who wants drinks?"

"Where'z the hossst?" Magnus slurred out between gulps of whiskey.

"Busy," I snapped back, my tone interrupting Barrett and Connor's conversation as they turned toward me.

"Okay, chill." Magnus blew out his cheeks. "In that case, I'll have a whiskey neat."

"Get it yourself, now," I yelled over the loud music, then walked out without waiting for another remark.

"Why did you fucking ask then?" I heard him shout out, but I was already heading toward the crowd where the bathrooms were.

Through the hundreds of people and with my height, it only took a moment to spot her in the corner beside the entrance. She stared back at me like she was waiting for me, but I couldn't read what she was thinking. All I knew was that I wanted to talk to her.

She folded her arms as soon as I walked closer. I pressed my hands against the wall so she stood between them, and I waited for her to speak first.

"What the fuck, Ari?"

"I could say the same thing," I countered.

She looked up at me, and I feared the worst, like at any moment, she was going to run. Instinctively, I put my other arm up so she was between me without room to escape.

"Is that what you really think about my work because you've said it a few times now."

"I don't give a shit about your work. I care about you." She pulled at the ends of her hair, uncertain how to respond.

"No, you don't. You can't. You aren't capable of that."

I sucked in a breath closing my eyes for a moment, but instead of rage, a sadness crept over my skin, chilling my blood.

"Come with me," I bellowed, and without waiting for her to respond, I held on to her hand, yanking her out of the club. It was time she knew the truth.

We hardly said two words to each other on the way back to the penthouse. I, for one, was consumed with the indescribable need to tell her what she saw wasn't the real me. And she was, well, just plain silent.

She threw her bag against the countertop and poured herself a drink of water from the kitchen tap.

"Now you have me here, what is it? If you think I'm going to roll around in the sheets with you, you're in cuckoo land."

"You keep saying I'm incapable of love. Why? Of all people, you should know not to judge a book by its cover. Sit."

"I'd rather stand," she said defiantly, keeping her distance.

"Sit down, Olivia, or I swear I will make you sit down myself."

My gaze leveled her, and she reluctantly sat. It was the furthest seat from me on the armchair.

The Ice Queen was back.

"Ever since we were introduced by our mutual friends, you have disliked me. I thought it was me. I even second-guessed myself. Sure I can be arrogant. I know that, but that isn't who I am."

"Don't forget womanizer."

I closed my eyes again, pushing away the hurt she hurled my way. "I should be so mad, and I was when you called me that. But the truth is, you don't understand me. You've never truly got to know me. Because you're afraid."

"I am not," she argued, sticking her chest out.

"You're the one who's so afraid of anything real in your life that you push it away."

"Did you pull me out of the club to give me a lecture? Thanks, but I have a dad that is fully capable of doing that."

I stared at her, and she held my gaze intently. This wasn't going exactly how I planned. I scratched my forehead and stood, pacing the suite's living room.

This seemed to quiet her down and allowed me time to gather my thoughts somewhat before I spoke again.

"Have you ever allowed yourself to be in love?"

She blinked quickly, and her cheeks bloomed with a rosy tinge of blush.

"No," she whispered. "But that's just mathematical. I haven't found the person yet. It's a numbers game, and I guess I haven't had enough lovers to find him yet." She arched an eyebrow defiant to the very end, but I expected nothing else.

I walked over to the window and stared out at the vast space below, lit up like a halogen lamp.

"I've slept around, I'm not denying that. Mostly for a decade, I have, but I am capable of more, much more." I hesitated as flashes of my past with Sophia came flooding back, but I needed Olivia to know that I was more than that. "I was engaged." She looked completely and utterly shocked as I turned around to find her.

"Really?"

"At twenty-three, my life was perfect. I'd met Sophia, and we'd fallen in love quickly and without hesitation. We spent all our days and nights together. She was perfect, and I'd met my match, so I proposed one day after we had a long lunch, and she said yes."

Burned in my memory was her face after I proposed. After getting down on one knee, she threw her arms around me with an ear-splitting grin—something ingrained like a permanent nightmare.

When I looked up at Olivia, curiosity etched on her face.

"So what happened then?" she asked, standing and walking toward me.

She stood opposite me, and I couldn't look at her for what was to come next. But I had this overwhelming need to tell her, and I didn't understand why.

"We were driving back home, and I was the happiest I have ever been. Out of nowhere, the rain started, and it got heavier really quickly. It was pelting down like rubber bullets. It was that hard. I took my eyes off the road for a second..." I paused. The pain clogged my throat suffocating my words.

"Oh, Ari, no." I felt her move closer.

"I swerved to avoid a pothole, and the last thing I remember was the car hydroplaning toward a tree. She didn't stand a chance."

My forehead pressed against the glass window, and I felt her fingers thread through mine. The connection instantly rendered me speechless.

"I'm so sorry, Ari." She tugged at my hand, imploring me to look at her. When I did, she held her hand up to my face and stroked it tenderly. I sucked in a level breath. "So you see, I am so much more than the man you perceive me to be, Olivia."

I put my hand up to hers and held it against my face.

She rolled her lips together and swallowed. Her eyes appeared glassy at my admission. "I know you are, and I'm sorry. I did not know about Sophia. If I had, I wouldn't have been so insensitive."

She held my gaze, and the silence between us was laced with an underlying emotion that hit my chest like an arrow to a bullseye.

"Why are you telling me this now?"

"Because whatever this is," I said. "It's more, much more,"
"I uh…"

"Olivia, please," I pleaded, and her gaze met mine. Closing the gap between us, I pulled her face to mine.

Saying nothing, she lifted her lips to mine and kissed me tenderly. I wrapped my hands around her waist and closing the gap, I deepened the kiss.

Her hands gripped the nape of my neck, and her kiss turned more desperate as our tongues clashed. Then her hands dipped down to my biceps.

I peeled my lips from hers, tracing the side of her neck and peppering her with gentle kisses. She took my hand and led me to the bedroom.

All without words.

When she stopped at the foot of the bed, she turned. Showing me her back, revealing the zipper to her dress. I lowered it slowly, running my hand down her exposed back as it dropped to her ankles. She turned to kick it away, and when her gaze hit mine, there was no mistaking the burning desire that mirrored mine.

Methodically, she unbuttoned my shirt, one by one, and I watched her, committing her face to memory as she did it. Her slight nose and long eyelashes framed her deep blue eyes and blonde hair that curled just underneath her jaw. I was captivated.

Trying to understand my feelings for this woman was beyond complicated.

I shouldered out of my shirt, and she ran her fingers down the wall of my chest to the button of my jeans. I stepped out of my jeans and underwear, unable to keep my hands off her any longer. Slipping my thumb between her thong and pelvis, I slid it down her thighs to her ankles, my hand stroking the back of her legs.

She took in a large lungful of air, then lay on the bed, and I followed, crawling up to meet her. I grazed my mouth across her belly button all the way up to the curve of her breasts. She moaned at the connection, and the sound made me thick with desire.

Impatiently, she pulled me up to her and kissed me with untamed passion. With my elbows bent, I balanced on top of her. Her breasts pushed into my chest. My dick rubbed against her opening, and I felt the warmth pool between her legs.

Breathless, she asked, "Are you clean?"

I looked up, surprised. "Yes, I had a doctor's appointment last week and have only been with you since."

"Then I want to feel you," she said, her eyes darkened.

"Fuck, Olivia, there is nothing more I want than to feel all of you." I took my lips to hers, and our tongues collided in an all-tongue kiss. I groaned in her mouth, the anticipation overriding all my senses.

She opened wider for me, and I rotated my hips, angling down my tip moistened with her arousal.

I pushed in about halfway, sinking into her slowly and stretching her until she was ready. I let out a throaty sound, her moist pussy too delicious for words. She moaned, her nails digging into my back, then with another thrust, she swallowed me whole.

I groaned at the feeling, taking my lips to hers in a breathless, wet kiss. Rotating my hips, I sunk into her again and again as heat scaled my back. Her hands fell around my ass, and she vaulted her hips upright, matching my intensity.

If there was any magic in this world, it was this woman right here. Losing myself, I continued thrusting into her. Her lips traced my jaw and neck, and the feeling heated my back.

She was close. I could feel her, see her skin flush with color. Her body tensed, and I couldn't hold mine anymore. She moaned, and I swallowed it with a kiss as we both found our release.

Lip-locked and out of breath, we reluctantly disentangled. I dipped my forehead to hers, and she stared at me longingly. Her hand palmed my cheek, and I leaned into it. "That was… nice." A smirk played on her delicious wet lips.

"It was perfect, like you," I added, lowering my lips to hers.

19

OLIVIA

Floored by his admission, I watched him sleep soundly beside me, jealous I wasn't able to do the same. I wanted to burst into tears when he told me his fiancé had died. But I held it together, barely. It's what I did. Always.

Growing up, when you were unsure if your mom was going to survive breast cancer or whether they would shut the electricity off or if we'd have to live off stale bread this week—well, that shit hardened you. So holding it together, that was just part of life.

I now understood why he flipped out last week on the drive to Carmichael Designs. He thought I might share the same fate as his fiancé when he was behind the wheel. It all made sense.

Then it didn't.

Because I'd never made love to anyone until now. It was the most beautiful, magical thing, but it was also the most terrifying. I was in my early thirties and here, lying beside me, was the magic I wasn't searching for, but somehow, in the disguise of an enemy, he was everything I needed.

But now? Why now? Was this the universe's way of saying

forget about your business? You're not good enough. Maybe you should just be a wife and be happy with that.

Wife? Heck, why did that just come into my mind. Ari wasn't thinking that, so why was I?

I shook my head at the outrageousness of it all, and he adjusted his head slightly.

Quickly, I stilled, not wanting him to wake from his slumber. Unable to reconcile what was on my mind, I gave up trying, gravitating to the warmth beside me.

* * *

"I got you, babe." Ari threaded his fingers through mine and pressed the palm of his hand reassuringly. I swallowed the lump in my throat as the jet roared on the tarmac, waiting for our late arrival. With a driver that disobeyed every law known to man, we arrived late, but we were here.

With every step I took ascending the jet's staircase, my heart pounded inside my rib cage, hammering like the roar of the twin jet engines.

On the top step, the air steward greeted us, and I barely heard a word she said. I was that into my head. *What would Lourde say? And Barrett? And why did it matter to me so damn much anyway?*

We rounded the corner, and I stilled behind Ari. Grateful for a millisecond, his body concealed our locked hands.

"Finally!" Connor said. Seated in rows of two, Connor and Barrett faced forward with Pepper and Lourde opposite them, their backs toward me. Behind them were Evelyn and Magnus engrossed in a conversation and had not yet noticed our arrival.

"What took so long?" Barrett asked. At the same time, Ari tugged on my hand, dragging me around to stand by his side, our hands intertwined for the world to see.

Barrett's eyes lowered to said hands.

"What the fuck?" Connor asked in a deathly whisper that made me immediately tense up.

"No way," Barrett scowled, looking at Ari, then across to me, confusion and disbelief spread across his knitted brows.

"What's all the commotion?" Pepper asked, disengaging from her conversation with Lourde and turning around in her seat.

Ari held up our conjoined hands, a smile set across his handsome face.

"Oh, hell yeah!" Pepper shrieked out, and Lourde craned her neck to get a better look. Her tone was enough to cause Magnus and Evelyn to stop chatting and look at us.

Sensing my shyness, he squeezed my hand a little tighter, pulling me close to him. He wrapped his hand around my waist, making me feel a little less awkward.

"She's my girl." He glared at Magnus. "She's mine."

Oh. Magnus' eyes widened and my erratic heart just skipped a beat.

I was terrified, but somehow, Ari's calm words and boyish jubilance had convinced me to tell our friends we were together.

Lourde stood, folding her arms across her body.

"Hold the goddamn phone." Lourde's high-pitched voice got the attention of the cabin. "You two hate each other?"

Ari looked at me with big brown eyes and a smile that made my walls crumble. I smiled back. Okay, so perhaps I melted that little bit more.

"We did," Ari said, kissing my hand.

"I wanted to stab him with a fork," I added, and it was met with laughter.

"Oh my God. I am in shock. How did this happen?" Lourde asked, taking her hands to her cheeks.

I shrugged, still uncertain myself how it happened.

"Must be the charm." Barrett laughed. "He was always a charmer."

"Boys, over there," Lourde said, grabbing me by the hand and directing me to sit opposite her. "I want to hear this too," Evelyn added, taking off her seat belt to kick her brother out of his seat.

"So you're separating us already?" Ari said. "I'm not sure I'm ok with that," he added, pulling a sad face in my direction.

I wanted to sit with Ari, on his lap preferably, but instead, Pepper, Lourde, and Evelyn had already buckled in and ready for a bedtime story aptly named how Ari and I went from wanting to kill each other to not being without one another.

So it was then that I proceeded to tell the girls how we evolved, leaving out the part about Ari and Sophia, his fiancé. I told them about our first week of work, how he worked me to the bone, closed doors on me, and made my life a living hell, which was met with horror by Lourde.

I had already told her all of this, but with her wedding preparations going on, it obviously had completely slipped her mind.

"I knew he'd been an asshole, but shit, I'm so sorry you had to deal with this all on your own," Lourde sympathized.

"It's fine. I put my big girl pants on and dealt with it. You know me." I picked up a cracker with some exotic French cheese and popped it into my mouth.

"I do, but Liv, sometimes it's okay not to be okay, you know?"

"You sound like a walking, talking billboard," Pepper stated, drinking her glass of bubbles.

"Well, it's true."

"I've not been okay for a while," Evelyn added, and we all turned her way. "With my injuries," she said after a pause. "Lourde's right, you know. Speak up. We are all here for you."

"It's just a bad day at work with an asshole boss." I looked over at Ari, and his eyes were fixed on me already.

He leaned forward in his seat. "Did you just call me an asshole?" A huge grin tipped on his full lips.

"Perhaps."

"What happened when you called me an asshole last time?" He took his hand and rested it on his chin. My cheeks heated, recalling the incident in Barrett's powder room.

"Hate sex is the best." Magnus spilled over into laughter, along with the rest of us.

Evelyn looked over at him disapprovingly.

"What, don't knock it till you've tried it," Magnus shared.

She shook her head.

"Barrett, can I please?" Lourde smiled, and I hadn't a clue what she was talking about.

He unclipped his seat belt and moved toward her. Then he bent down and whispered something in her ear, and a huge smile leaped from her cheeks.

"So we were going to ask you guys something when we were in Vegas, but with people disappearing or getting hammered at dinner, we just couldn't find the right time, so…"

She looked up at Barrett adoringly, and he pulled her into his side.

"We would love you all to be part of our bridal party."

"Well, finally!" Pepper shrieked out. "Took you forever to ask!"

Pepper and Evelyn, I understood, but me? I was deeply humbled by her request. "I'd love to be your bridesmaid."

Evelyn unclipped her belt and gave her soon-to-be sister-in-law a huge hug. The boys all hooted and cheered.

Lourde turned to me. "So now I can partner you with Ari!" Lourde clapped her hands together. "This couldn't be more perfect than if it were a screenplay." Her grin stretched across her porcelain skin.

"Eve, you and I are hitched then?" Magnus tossed her a wink.

"Gosh, is he always like that?" Evelyn turned her focus from Magnus to the girls and Barrett, who was still sitting by Lourde's side.

"He is, but he will behave, won't you, Magnus?" Barrett clarified. "It is my sister, after all."

He blew out a puff of air between his cheeks. "Behave is my middle name!"

Ari and Connor laughed. Barrett didn't.

"Just like you behaved with my sister?" Connor added.

Barrett smiled, pulling Lourde in for a kiss.

My gaze met Ari's, and more than anything, I wanted him to come sit by me, but instead, he remained in his chair.

"And there's one more thing," Barrett said. "We moved the wedding up."

"How can you with the venue? Isn't it booked out? Pepper asked as we all knew full well how hard Lourde has been battling wedding venues.

Most of them were hammering to have a Diamond wedding at their venue, but Lourde was too indecisive to choose.

"Well, we changed venues. We are getting married in the Hamptons next month." Barrett took her hand in his.

Evelyn leaned forward after returning to her seat. "Are you expecting?"

"No way, she would have told me." Pepper flapped her hand, dismissing the idea completely.

But come to think of it...

"You weren't drinking," I added.

A smile peeled on both their lips. "We are pregnant." Lourde squealed out in exuberance.

"Arghh!"

"Oh my God!"

Shrieks and cheers erupted inside the cabin, and we were all out of our seats, congratulating Barrett and Lourde.

Connor and Magnus slapped him on the back, "My friend, you're going to be a dad," Connor said.

"Why didn't you tell us!" Pepper squealed.

"We just wanted to get past the early stages. It was so hard not to tell you guys, believe me. But Barrett wanted me to wait till the ultrasound."

She turned to face me. "That's why I have been so useless with helping you and the business. I've been so sick. Morning sickness is shit! One minute you're hungry, the next, you want to barf up a lung."

I pulled her in for a hug. "I don't care about that. I can manage work. You focus on yourself now and that little bundle of joy growing inside for you."

"Is it a boy or a girl?" Evelyn asked, so excited to be an aunty for the first time.

"We don't know yet," Lourde said, and Magnus rolled his eyes. "You will not be one of those couples who wait for a surprise, are you?"

"Hell, no," Barrett said. "We find out in the next ultrasound."

After we congratulated them, the chatter resumed to a normal decibel after all the excitement. I noticed Ari fade into the background, quiet and withdrawn. Not enough to warrant the attention of others, but it was definitely something I noticed.

I hopped out of my seat to where he sat, staring at his phone.

"How exciting for them," I said, sitting on the arm of the chair.

"So exciting," he uttered, but the smile didn't reach his mocha eyes.

"Everything okay?" My hand slid down his corded forearms, wrapping around his fingers. He gently squeezed my hand, and a feeling of relief flooded through me.

"Fine, just catching up on emails before we land." He picked up his phone again and started flicking through. I didn't need any more of a hint than that, so I stood and released his hand.

"I'll leave you to it then." I turned to go back to my seat, but he reached for my wrist. "Hey, I had fun this weekend," he said, and there was a finality to his tone I didn't think I was imagining.

"Me too." I offered a tight smile before quickly retreating to my seat.

Absentmindedly, I nodded and agreed when talk of baby nurseries and clothes were thrown around, and for the rest of the trip, I counted the minutes until we landed.

Not once had Ari looked up again at me. Glued to his phone like it was an extension of his arm, he focused on that and nothing else. When the guys finally picked up on his mood, I overheard him say he had work to do.

Work? Now?

Had he regretted us, or did he actually have something pressing?

I gripped the seat when the plane descended, not because I was afraid of flying but because I was angry. A boiling rage had quietly heated for the rest of the plane trip, and now we were coming to land. I was angry. At myself first for allowing myself to take my eye off the prize and let my guard down. Completely down.

Well, come tomorrow, my walls would be firmly in place. After all, I was in control of my feelings and my reactions, and it was time I remembered that.

20

ARI

I woke up with an epic hangover. I'd done it again, drowned my sorrows with a bottle of whiskey, wanting to forget. Wanting to push the pain away that had consumed me on the flight home.

And in withdrawing during the flight, I had pushed Olivia away. The one person who had made me feel alive again and made me believe in love.

After a scorching shower and three Tylenol—because two would not cut it—I arrived at the store on Madison Avenue. Late, but there.

Olivia buzzed around from trade to trade, ensuring the installation was running like clockwork. Contractors busily put the finishing touches on cabinetry while electricians got to work on hanging the enormous chandelier over the entrance. Ice Queen to the last word, she was a woman on a mission, and knowing that, I tried to steer away as much as possible. But damn, it was hard, especially when the blouse she had on was sheer enough to see the rose pink lace bra underneath. I wasn't the only one to notice. Rex Carmichael was certainly paying her more attention than he needed, making my blood boil that much more.

I didn't have to be here. Actually, it was worse than a hammer to the head to be in her vicinity, especially around a flirty Rex I wanted to sucker punch in the gut and never-ending power tools. But with Grandmama arriving shortly, I didn't have a choice. She wanted to see me.

As the morning burned into lunch, my hangover slowly retreated. Consumed by work, it didn't stand a chance with all the chaos going on. Time to rest was nonexistent when the store was launching in just five days on Friday, and there was still so much to do.

The design was one thing, but stock, marketing, and merchandise were another. Sanella was across it as was I.

As much as it pained me to admit it, Sanella had been the solid rock by Grandmama in my decade-long absence. When it should have been me by her side supporting her in the family business, he had stepped up. Perhaps working for him would be the best thing when Grandmama retired.

I picked up a piece of wire hidden behind boxes. A clear and dangerous hazard had someone stepped on it. A vein ticked in my neck as I immediately saw red.

"Hey, listen up," I yelled out over the power tools. I waited until everyone was silent and all eyes were on me. Olivia stood, folding her arms across her chest, waiting for me impatiently.

"Anyone, and I mean anyone, who leaves shit like this on the floor again…" I held up the spindly sharp wire for everyone to see, "… I will fire you."

Quietness echoed around the previous hive of activity, and Olivia just stared at me slack-jawed.

I was the first to turn away. Walking outside, I threw the wire in the trash bin just outside the front doors. I exhaled, then turned to the sky. "Sophia, please give me the strength I need to get through the day."

A finger of light filtered between the buildings opposite, and warmth surrounded me.

When I looked back down, Grandmama's car had just pulled up. Before her driver could open her door, I stepped forward and lifted the handle on the passenger side.

She looked up. "Darling."

"Grandmama, let me help you out." I stepped onto the street and looped my hand under her elbow to assist her. When she stepped onto the sidewalk, a rouge photographer appeared.

"Farrah, Ari, how about a photo, please?" The man with square glasses that looked like they were for show rather than for enhanced vision held his camera to his face.

"Of course." Grandmama smoothed down her hair and was pose-ready. I stood, legs apart, and offered a meek smile.

"Amazing, thank you!" He retreated, allowing Grandmama to take me in.

"You look awful, Aristotle," she surmised.

I shrugged. "Vegas," I said, wanting to steer her off the scent of my downward spiral.

Gripping her walking stick, she cast her watchful eyes over me. "I see," she maintained. Not completely convinced by my answer, she ambled into the store.

As soon as she walked through, the contractors recognized her and immediately kept their heads down. Diligent and hardworking, they persisted, knowing that doing a good job would keep them on Farrah's payroll for years to come.

While she made her rounds with the contractors, I was going to tend to my emails, but when I was about to start, Farrah called me over. She stood with Olivia, and damn, there was no way I could avoid her now.

I walked over and brushed down my jacket and pants.

"So, now I have you both here. I wanted to say this store is truly something else."

Olivia stared at her. "It will be. We are nearly there."

"You two are a formidable team," she remarked, staring at Olivia, then me.

Olivia blushed slightly, then swallowed. "Thank you, Farrah," she said, "Now if you don't mind, I was going to check on the fixtures upstairs."

"I do," she said, and Olivia stopped, tilting her head to the side.

"I mind because I have lunch booked at Osteria for the three of us."

Her eyes darted to me, then clearing her throat, she addressed Grandmama, "I think I should stay here and keep an eye on things. Why don't you two go?"

"I think she's right, Grandmama," I agreed, unsure of where we stood and thinking that lunch with my grandmother wasn't a good place to find out, especially since the woman was more clued in than Sherlock Holmes.

"Nonsense, I've got my foreman here. I'll just let him know I'm borrowing you both for an hour."

"Pedro?" she yelled, then Pedro immediately rose, meeting her, so she didn't have to walk too far to meet him. Olivia stood, playing with the ends of her hair, staring anywhere but at me.

How could you want to spend time with someone, then dread it at the same time?

"Things have been chaotic around here, haven't they?" I asked, trying to keep things light.

"Sure have."

"Listen, before Farrah gets back, I just wanted to say I'm going through some stuff at the moment, and I'm sorry things are the way they are after our weekend. It wasn't my intention."

She looked up at me. "Perhaps it's best if we just leave things amicable between us, Ari. No hard feelings, you know?"

The words hit me like a train, but I couldn't stop them, and I certainly couldn't respond.

She looked up at me expectantly, but when I was about to say something, Farrah returned.

"It's sorted then."

"I guess it is," Olivia said and looked up at me, a sadness behind her eyes replaced quickly by her professionalism.

She walked off ahead toward the entrance and picked up her bag. Farrah looked at me but said nothing. There wasn't a damn thing anyone could say to replace the dread building inside me and the fact that she had just broken up with me.

Worse still, I didn't stop her.

21

OLIVIA

She wasn't wrong when she said this was her favorite restaurant. Osteria restaurant was a landmark in Manhattan, an institution for decades, but of course, I'd never been.

Not because I hadn't wanted to try it, but because every cent I had, I gave back to Mom and Dad, paying off their loan so that they didn't have a cloud hanging over their heads during retirement. I'd given up a place of my own so that they could have theirs. So when it came to spending hundreds of dollars at a fancy restaurant, thank you, next.

But this saffron casarecce with braised Wagyu shin and salted ricotta had me forgetting momentarily about Ari and kicking myself that I hadn't tried this place sooner.

"So now we've discussed the store opening. Tell me, how was Vegas? The last time I went to Vegas, I woke up in a suite full of hungover models, a chimpanzee, and a python in the kitchen."

I burst into laughter, and Ari shook his head like he'd heard this story before. "It sounds like that movie *The Hangover!*"

"That was a lion," Ari chimed in.

"But a chimpanzee?" I questioned.

Farrah shrugged. "The zoo was in town." Then added, "I think, but I can't be sure."

"Did you fair as bad as my grandson over here?" Farrah questioned, and the truth was, upon seeing Ari arrive late at the store this morning, I couldn't believe my eyes.

Disheveled to those who knew him, bags held at the base of his eyes while he reeked of a brewery when he passed by. So last night, he drank. And drank some more. Had he regretted everything between us? It seemed that way, and I pushed away the knife twisting in my gut.

"I pulled up okay," I said, keen to change the subject.

"I see, so it was just Ari then." She stared at him, assessing, and he stared right back, his hand on the glass in front of him.

Taking his scotch to his lips, he shrugged. "When in Vegas."

"And at lunch?" I threw back, unable to help myself.

He gazed up at me, and there was a pause at the table. Immediately, I regretted saying it not because of Ari but because Farrah was now staring directly at me. I could apologize, but there was no point. It was already out there.

She turned to face Ari. "Olivia's right. Take the rest of the day off, Aristotle."

Without an argument, he stood. Raising his arm, he finished the rest of the liquid, tilting his head back to get every drop.

"Fine," he said, kissing Farrah on the forehead, then turned to leave, his steak untouched.

I swallowed down the lump in my throat.

"I'm sorry, I shouldn't have said that."

"Really?" She looked up at me. "Because you don't strike me as the type to apologize." Farrah widened her eyes.

I breathed out, the emotion coming out of nowhere.

"Let me tell you something about Aristotle, Olivia."

I shuffled in my seat, unsure what she knew or if I was jumping to conclusions.

"He is loyal to a fault but has had some dark days in his life."

"I know," I breathed out on a thread of whisper.

Surprised by my admission, she leaned forward. "He's told you about Sophia?"

"Yes, and I can't imagine how painful that must have been."

She stared at me for a moment then like a light bulb had gone off in her head, she said, "That was you in his room in Vegas, wasn't it?"

Oh God.

"You're the reason he is a changed man. I knew it. I knew there was something there from the minute you walked into Farrah and the moment he said he loathed you."

Loathed me?

Well, okay, still hearing it hurt, but she knew now, and all professionalism was gone out the frigging window.

"It wasn't my intention, I… I…"

"Loathed my grandson too?"

I looked back up to see a wide-eyed Farrah, deep-set wrinkles around her eyes awaiting my response. "Yes," I admitted in an almost whisper.

"Well, well. All I can say is thank you," she said.

"No, I don't think that's necessary."

"Why? I haven't seen him this happy and focused since Sophia. And if it's not you, then who is it?"

Dumbstruck, I toyed with the leftover pasta on my plate, not feeling hungry anymore. Was what we had real, and if it was, why had it all disappeared, like I was nothing at all?

Although sensing my discomfort, she said, "He is a complicated man. Sophia was his everything, and he only started his playboy ways after he fell into a hole of despair. But he has an enormous heart, and one that is truly rare, Olivia. I don't know what's going on between you two but whatever it is, stick with it."

"Farrah, the truth is, I don't know what's going on either. We are fire and fire."

"That's a good thing. Just give him time. Don't give up on him."

"He's giving up on me," I admitted, and a weird feeling came over me. One which took me by surprise so much so that I had to shake it off literally and realize who I was speaking with. "You don't need to hear any of this." I straightened in my seat.

"But I do." She reached over and put her hand on mine. Her fingers, although bony and bent, provided some unusual comfort. "Olivia, you remind me so much of myself. Strong, determined, and fiercely intelligent. Don't let that fire end up costing you love."

"I'm not in love." I laughed aloud, and she regarded me intently. Doubt ricochet off my chest hitting me in the face. *Was I in love with Ari?*

"Well, I once was. And he was the most handsome man that existed on the planet," she shared, removing her hand from mine and reaching for the napkin in her lap, then dotting the outskirts of her mouth with it. She delicately pushed her cutlery together and let out a heavy sigh, one full of backstory.

"What was his name?" I inquired, not imagining Farrah ever having room for a man in her busy life.

"Carlo. Carlo Bugsetti. We met in Rome when I was starting out sourcing material in Rome. He was the son of a lace supplier. We had a whirlwind romance. He took me to Tuscany. We drove in a convertible with the roof off and drank wine from the wineries in Siena." She sighed. "He was my everything."

"But then I chose my career, and I can't be mad about that

because look where I am," she said, looking around. But there was a melancholy in her voice that was undeniable.

"Like you, Olivia, I came from hardship. My parents, like yours, had no money."

"How do you know about my family?" I asked, taken aback.

"Because your parents used to clean my house."

"What did you say?" I asked.

"They didn't tell you?" She looked at me, perplexed.

"No. Mom and Dad never mentioned it." They knew I was working at FGC. *Why would they leave that out?*

"You used to come with them because they couldn't afford daycare, and, of course, I didn't mind."

I blinked back at her. Was this the truth? And why was I the last to know?

"Not only that, you and Ari used to play together sometimes when he was at my place."

"Wait, the mansion on the upper east side was yours?"

"Yes."

"I used to think it was Christmas going there each week." I lowered my head. "And that boy that shared his toys with me was Ari?" I cried, almost bordering on tears. "Does he know this?"

"No, he doesn't."

"Wait, is that why you hired me? You felt sorry for me?" I sure as hell didn't want anyone's pity, and the possibility made me warm with frustration.

"Do you think I built an empire by taking pity on people? Don't insult me, Olivia." She leveled me with her eyes. "I picked you because I recognized something you had. It was drive, a commitment to excellence. You can only get that from struggling. I struggled, and I know your family struggled. I also know you're doing everything you can for them."

"How do you know all of this, Farrah?"

"Because I invest in people. And the people I surround myself with, I look into."

I shook my head in disbelief. "So you know about my parents' investment?"

"Yes. When they didn't turn up one day, I called your father, but he didn't answer. Eventually, I found out about the poor investment he made and that he was in over his head. I offered to help him, but he wouldn't hear me. He had too much pride to accept help from me. That pride is in you."

I was fidgeting now, interlacing my fingers and rubbing them against one another as I tried to process everything she had just told me.

"I don't know what to say. This is all very strange. Why are you telling me this?"

She drew in a deep breath. "Because I know struggle, and I once knew love. I let one go, and I regret it every damn day. Don't be like me, Olivia. Give Aristotle a chance, please."

I held her gaze. There was something in her eyes that moved me. I cared for Ari so much, but there was something inside him he had to figure out first.

"What happened with Carlo?" I asked.

"He got married, had children, and is living his best life," she said wistfully. Then, raising her hand, she signaled the waiter for the check.

"I see."

"I hope so, dear."

I nodded. "I just need some time and so does he."

"What for?"

"Things were great in Vegas, but since the plane ride home, he has been different."

"What exactly did he tell you about Sophia?"

The waiter came over, and she gave him her credit card without looking at the bill in the binder.

"Well, he told me she was his fiancée, and after proposing,

they were driving and that an accident happened, and she passed away."

She nodded, and I got the feeling there was more to the story, more that he had left out.

"Is there something else I should know?"

"Just give him time, Olivia. He is a good man, a man with a heart of gold. Promise me you won't give up on him yet."

Promise? This was strange and not at all what I expected when I agreed to come to lunch. But here I was about to make a promise to my boss that I wasn't going to give up on her grandson.

"I promise," I said with a slight apprehension in my voice.

"Good, now come along. We don't want to leave the contractors for too long."

"Yes, of course."

* * *

The afternoon buzzed with progress, but I couldn't get out of my mind the conversation I had with Farrah at lunch.

When things had quieted down, I took the first opportunity to step out and call Dad.

After a few rings, he picked up.

"Olivia!"

"Dad," I quipped

"What's wrong?" he asked.

"Why didn't you tell me when I started working for Farrah that you used to clean her house?"

"Oh, that."

"Yes, oh that!" I said, exasperated and pulling into an alcove so no one could hear my conversation.

"Well, I was hoping she wouldn't remember you and me."

"You were what?"

"You were three years old, and we were only cleaned her house for six months. I didn't think she'd remember."

"You didn't think she'd remember?"

"Sorry, I probably should have told you."

"Yes, you should have!"

"But would that have changed anything if you knew?"

"Probably not," I admitted realizing I should probably take it a bit easier on my old man.

"She was so lovely, Farrah, and she had a grandson you were in love with!"

"What?"

"You were both the same age, and you used to play with him and cry bullets when we had to leave."

"Ari," I breathed out.

"Aristotle, that's right. How do you remember his name?"

"Because he is my boss," I said, exasperated.

"Oh, we are really coming full circle now." Dad laughed, and I groaned out, unsure what to make of all of this.

"What's wrong, kiddo?"

"Nothing, Dad," I said, shaking my head.

"I just wish you'd told me, that's all. I've been blindsided by a few things lately."

"Sorry, Livvy, but tell me what else is troubling you."

I pulled the received close. "Ari and I had a thing, but now we don't, Farrah knows, and it's really a mess."

"Boss Ari?"

"Uh-huh."

"Well, I'd like to meet the man. You should bring him to the house, and your momma will make him her boeuf bourguignon."

I put my hand up to my forehead. "Dad, I don't think that's a good idea."

"Are you embarrassed? I taught you never to be embarrassed about your upbringing."

"I'm not embarrassed, Dad. Funny thing is, I think you'd like him, actually."

"Then what is it?"

"I think we just need some time to figure out if we are right together and if a relationship is what I need at this point in my life."

"Darling, you are thirty-three. If not now, when?"

"Jesus, thanks, Dad," I scolded. "Anyway, I have to go, we have the store opening for Farrah in less than three days, and I have a store full of contractors I am meant to be watching."

"Go. But I want to meet the man."

I let out a sigh. "Bye, Dad."

"Bye, sweets."

I trudged off inside the store, confusion clouding my brain. I was determined to make this store opening the best store opening in Manhattan, and as it was coming to an end, deep down, I was more uncertain than I'd ever been. When it was my work that had provided me the security and safety I craved, I was scared to no end, and that virgin territory I didn't like.

22

ARI

My driver dropped me home but not before stopping to buy me a bottle of whiskey.

By the time I looked up, the bottle was nearly empty, and it was dark outside.

Pain burned in my chest like a hole unable to be mended. I'd blown it with Olivia, the one person who made me feel something again.

But I couldn't do a damn thing about it. The memory of Sophia was too hurtful to ignore.

And the announcement of Lourde and Barrett having a baby was enough for the grief I had buried to spill to the surface. When I thought I was clear of the hurt, it just pushed me back down again, drowning me in my fear and loneliness.

I reached for the rest of the bottle and poured it, missing half the glass. It spilled all over my pants.

Fuck.

Emotion overpowered me, and sadness turned into anger. I grabbed the bottle and smashed it against the floorboards.

Fear enshrouded me when she had gotten close. When I

had what I had with Sophia, or better if I was honest, but I couldn't think that.

I stumbled to where the shattered bottle lay in pieces. Shards of glass like a puzzle needing to be glued back together stared back at me. I picked up the pieces one by one. Then one sliced my finger.

"Fuck," I yelled out as blood poured from the cut.

It didn't help, I didn't feel any pain, but the sight of blood curdled my insides.

Resolved to leave it be, I stumbled to the kitchen, finding a tea towel and wrapping it around the bloodied finger.

The agony in my heart was too much. I walked back to the couch and fell on it.

The next thing I knew, I had passed out cold.

***

It was a buzzing sound that woke me, and I jerked upright. The motion made my head spin.

I looked around. What time was it? My head hurt like a motherfucker, and I was still in my shirt and suit pants. My stomach growled and lurched into my throat. As I got up to stand, I spotted the shattered bottle, and everything came flooding back.

The buzzer sounded again, and I yelled back, knowing they couldn't hear, "I'm coming."

I pressed the intercom button.

"What?" I yelled into the receiver down to the concierge.

"Sir, I have Victoria here to see you."

"Victoria?"

"Yes, sir, you asked me to let you know when she arrived."

"I did?" I questioned, not remembering that entire conversation he claimed we had. But Jay, my concierge, said nothing.

"What would you like me to do, sir?"

"Send her up," I said, knowing that turning her away would be a dick move.

I went to the bathroom and splashed my face full of water. The cold woke me up like a slap to the cheeks and dulled down my headache, so it was barely manageable. The last time I saw Victoria was when Olivia turned me down in Barrett's bathroom, and I went home wishing it was Olivia I was inside of, not her. We had a fling, but that was that. I checked my watch. It was nine o'clock at night. *What was she doing here now?*

I heard the elevator doors open and walked out into the living area to greet her. My legs felt heavy, and my stomach growled even louder.

Dressed in a stunning violet dress and sky-high heels that elongated her already pencil-thin legs, she strutted into the penthouse toward me.

"There he is," she cooed as I walked toward her. She wrapped her arms around me and kissed me on both cheeks.

"Victoria. What are you doing here?"

She jerked back. "You invited me over. I have to say I was surprised to get your call, you know because you don't do relationships."

I scratched my head, trying to think when I made the call to her.

"You smell like a bar, Ari. Everything all right?"

"No, Yes. I don't know." I shook my head.

She stared at me curiously, and I contemplated telling her about Olivia, then stopped myself from telling one of the most indiscreet models in Manhattan about my life.

"I'm sorry I called you. I honestly don't remember doing that. It's been a rough day."

"I see. Well, you have me here now. The least you can do is offer me a glass of wine."

"Victoria," I said in a warning.

Her lips twisted into a glint of a smirk.

"It's not happening, hun."

"Oh, honey, why not? Last time was incredible!"

That's because I imagined you were someone else.

But she posed a good question, *why not?* Here was another model gagging to climb aboard my dick, and I was turning her down with no thought or contemplation.

"I just can't."

She dragged her eyes down to the zipper of my pants. "But maybe he can?"

I let out a laugh. "Let's have lunch soon," I said. "As friends?"

I pulled her in for a hug, "Ah, I should hate you, but I can't, Ari Goldsmith. You're just too darn nice."

"Don't worry, others do," I said, thinking about how I left things with Olivia. I'd practically ignored her the entire day. Then lunch came back like a blinding mistake.

She huffed, her attention drifting to the nearby table. "For the road?" I said, reaching over and gifting her the vintage bottle Cristal.

She shrugged. "Well, if you insist."

I laughed and walked behind her toward the lift.

She sashayed her hips back and forth, and I shook my head. "Magnus would shoot me dead between the eyes for sending you away."

"How is Maggy?"

"Same, separated and sleeping his way around town. You know."

"There's a rumor going around that he is buying Sadie's."

"The strip clubs?"

"Uh-huh."

I laughed aloud. I pressed the elevator button and kissed her on the cheek. "That's the funniest thing I've heard."

"It's true."

I tilted my head to the side. "Who told you that?"

"I don't kiss and tell."

"Well, I think your sources are wrong this time, Victoria. Magnus hasn't worked since his parents sold the tech company and made billions."

The door opened, and she walked inside. Turning, she blew me a kiss. "My sources are never wrong." She winked, then she was gone.

My reflection was all I saw after the doors closed. Hair disheveled and bags under my eyes, my shirt crumpled like paper. I looked like I did all those years ago when I'd hit rock bottom.

After I took a long shower and stuffed my face full of carbohydrates, I felt mildly better. When I lay on my bed, distraction played its part for so long until the loneliness crept in. I contemplated further distraction and calling Magnus to find out about the rumors Victoria was talking about, but I wasn't in the mood. I wanted to call Olivia to tell her I had pushed her away because I was scared.

Scared of losing her.

Scared of falling for her.

Scared to lose someone I loved all over again.

I buried my head in the pillow, and when I woke up, it was morning. Gazing down, I found my phone in my hand and light streaming through the large glass window.

I changed and was tempted to have another drink to ward off the pain getting a grip on me yet again. But work waited for no one, especially today when I was meeting with the forensic investigators about the missing money of Farrah's fortune. A drink would have to wait.

23

OLIVIA

It was after lunch when I decided to take a break and go outside to fetch a coffee.

I hadn't heard from or seen Ari since he bailed on our lunch on Monday. It was now Thursday. What did I expect? A call, a hundred red roses with an apology?

As if.

I walked to my favorite coffee shop on Madison Avenue, desperate for a caffeine fix.

"Triple espresso, please."

"Triple today, Olivia?" the barista questioned as he peered at me over his thick black rims.

"It's a triple kinda day."

"Coming right up," he said, busily navigating the orders ahead of me.

I tapped my card, then floated to the side, along with the other people waiting. On their phones, heads down, they were in the zone. The work zone where I should have been, but clearly, I wasn't. I was still trying to make heads and tails of what Farrah said.

The store was due to open tomorrow, and everything was

just about in order. I was finessing now, my favorite part. The contractors had finished, and the first delivery of gowns came in this morning. I'd inspected the guest list, and my heart fluttered. Fashion leaders, celebrities, supermodels, and only the best editors from *Vogue* and *Glamour* were going to be in attendance.

But I kept thinking about the boy I played with as a little girl. The boy who had captured my heart back then and now thirty years later. Farrah had made me promise not to give up on him. On us. But I didn't think there was an *us* anymore. He had abandoned me like I was just another one of his flings, and the pain cut deeper than I'd like to admit.

"Olivia," the barista called like it was his second time calling, and I immediately looked up and out of my head. "Sorry." I stepped forward and wrapped both hands around the coffee.

"No probs, you have a great day now."

"Thanks."

"Come back soon." He winked, and I let out a smile before quickly retreating. Allowing myself to flirt back wasn't even on my radar, not anymore.

I walked the busy sidewalk, making my way back to the store. Car horns and bustling streets fell into the background, and as I looked up, I saw Ari.

He smiled slightly, but again it didn't reach his eyes. Like a colleague smiling at another colleague. Platonic. It hurt, but I did the same, smiling back.

"Olivia," he greeted, opening the front door to let me inside.

"Thanks," I said and slid straight past him, careful not to touch him on the way in.

Stepping inside, I moved to the side to let him see the progress since he hadn't been back all week. So much had happened. With the contractors gone, a thorough clean, and half of the beautiful gowns adorning the custom-made coat hangers, it looked completely transformed.

"This is... just wow," he said, marveling at the achievement I'd pulled off in such a short time.

I looked around too. It looked phenomenal. I'd transformed a dull store into a modern, sophisticated flagship store in just three weeks. Stunning woods crafted by the finest craftsmen lightened the space. The little-known designer, Rex Carmichael, had one more day of being an unknown. When the launch hit tomorrow, he would be a secret no more.

Then there were the glass display boxes used to highlight featured shoes and jewels. Accents of deep purples and gold were weaved throughout the store, working symbiotically with the high-end brand of FGC.

A chandelier with soft yellow light hung over the large void in the entrance, and elegantly opposite the entrance was *'Farrah Goldsmith Couture'* in large cursive gold metal signage.

It was a masterpiece and the first of many.

He tilted his head to the side, taking me in, and I gazed up at him. "I'm so proud of you," he said.

"Thank you," I admitted graciously, taking his praise for once and not biting back. "Have you spoken to Farrah?"

"No, but I have a two o'clock with her."

"I see."

Did that mean he still didn't know I was the little girl who played with him all those years ago?

"Why? Is everything all right?"

I blew out a puff of air. "Everything's just fine, Ari." I stalked off. If he would not address us, then I had better things to do than worry about Ari Goldsmith.

We were so done. Being invisible wasn't my style. And regardless of my promise to one of the most powerful women in Manhattan, I would not be a ghost to Ari Goldsmith or anyone else.

24

ARI

There was nothing more I wanted to tell her than how conflicted I was. How much I needed her but couldn't reach out and touch her. I was afraid, afraid of what I felt. But as I watched her walk away, so did a piece of my heart. Her feet pounded the floor as she quickly created distance between us, and yet again, I was unable to stop her. She'd just quit on me for good now.

Pain formed in my chest like blockwork, and I wanted it to disappear.

I went to my meeting with Grandmama, focusing on work rather than being dragged away into the darkness. Being day drunk was tempting, but it could wait until after Farrah.

When I walked into her office, she looked up from her screen.

"Sorry, I have been in meetings all week. With the launch tomorrow, I honestly don't know if I've ever been busier."

She pushed off the armrests of her chair to a standing position. "Grandmama, don't get up, please." Quickly, I walked around her desk to where she was struggling to stand and kissed her cheeks, one then the other.

I retreated to the chair opposite and flopped into it. "Well, I have some good news," I said, trying to sound excited.

"I was hoping you would. Tell me everything."

"Sanella is your thief along with Drummond from accounting. They have funneled cash off and into multiple accounts over the last three years and more aggressively over the last year."

She paused, soaking in what I just said, then suddenly, her face morphed into a fire I'd only ever seen a handful of times. With one clumsy push, she threw her entire stack of papers off the desk in a fit of rage.

"Calm down," I said, not wanting her to give herself a heart attack.

She slammed her fist on the table. "Calm down?" Her nostrils flared. "That son of a bitch."

The door opened, and I turned back to find her assistant in the doorway.

"Is everything all right?" she asked, alarm flickering across her face as she took in the mess.

The papers floated into a heap on the floor, along with her folders and stationery. It was a chaotic mess.

"Fine, leave us," Farrah scolded, not bothering to look up.

The office door quickly shut behind me.

"I started this company with nothing. *Nothing*," she yelled. "Why would he do this?"

"I don't know, Grandmama. The usual reasons like greed and ego come to mind." I shook my head. "Who knows why people do anything," I offered. "I always got a bad vibe from him since day one."

"You have always said that. I should have listened to you." She let out a sigh, her anger now diluted into action. "So what now?"

"I've organized the detectives to take him in, quietly, of course."

"When?"

I looked at the dial on my Patek Phillipe watch. "They should be here in thirty minutes."

"Plain clothed?"

"Of course," I said.

"Good, I hope he gets the book thrown at him."

"You probably won't recover the millions. You know that."

"Oh, I will. I will not let that snake take my money with him. I will seize every possession that asshole has down to his bloody socks and underwear if I have to."

"There's my grandmama." I smiled, her drive reminding me of Olivia. My smile soon faded into sadness as the memory of what we could have had burned into my mind.

"What is it?" When I looked up, Grandmama was staring at me, concerned about her weathered face.

"Nothing. Let's go pay the asshole a visit, shall we?" I got up to stand, ready to take the son of a bitch down.

"Wait, Aristotle. Sit back down." Her tone told me we were not done, and when she spoke that way, I knew it was something important. I did as she requested of me and sat down.

"Do you remember when you were a little boy, you played in my apartment all the time?"

What was the woman talking about? Had dementia finally crept in after all these years?

"Of course, I do. Ah, but why would you want to talk about this now?"

"Oh, hush. There was a little girl who you played with. She used to come over when her parents cleaned the house."

Immediately I remembered the little girl with long blonde hair in pigtails and an infectious giggle. "Yes, of course, we used to play hide and seek together, and I think I cried when she left, didn't I?"

"You cried for days when she never came back too. I thought I had to organize a shrink for you. It was that bad."

"Okay, okay," I said. "What's your point, Grandmama."

"Do you remember her name?"

I wracked my brains, but for the life of me, I couldn't remember her name, just her rosy cheeks and plaited pigtails. "Nope, not a clue."

My grandmama smiled, her veneer teeth white as chalk. "Her name, Aristotle, was Olivia Willows."

"No, it wasn't," I countered immediately.

But my grandmama just watched me while I stared at her vacantly.

Those same blue eyes.

Ash blonde hair.

Pointy nose.

Fuck me. It was her.

"How is that possible?"

"Her parents had a cleaning company, lovely people they were. You were so fond of Olivia then as you are now."

I shook my head. "I'm in shock, that's all."

"I see."

"Why are you telling me this now rather than interrogating the asshole, Sanella?"

"Because for once, I'm choosing love over work. Over my obligation."

I raised my eyebrows in a question, my stomach churning with emotion. "Does she know?"

"I told her at lunch on Monday after I sent you home. I've been meaning to tell you, but things have just been crazy, and I didn't know she was the cause of your change until Monday when I saw you both together."

My hands fell around the arms of the chair, my hands gripping the leather. "It doesn't matter if I knew her back then."

"No, it doesn't. But what matters is how you feel now. Grandson, I know you, I know what Sophia's death did to you, and I also know that Olivia has brought you back. She's made you reclaim part of yourself that was missing for so long. She is your match."

Every muscle in my body tensed at her words.

"No, she's not," I said, pushing away the pain welling in my chest.

She leaned forward in her seat. "You need to forgive yourself so you can love again."

I got up to stand. "I appreciate you telling me all of this, but I'm fine. What we had was a fling and nothing more. Now let's go before the detectives arrive."

She got up to stand, leaning on the desk for support. I made my way over to her and looped her arm into mine. "Don't let her go, Aristotle."

I gripped her tighter and pursed my lips. With my jaw set, I channeled my bubbling anger into the man on the opposite side of the floor.

Sanella.

When we arrived at his office, I asked his assistant to meet the impending guests in the foyer and, when they arrived, to lead them straight in.

My grandmama straightened beside me, then pushed open the door and stepped in.

Sanella looked up from his computer screen. "Farrah." His gaze looked beyond her to me.

"And Ari, to what do I owe the pleasure?" He looked back down at his computer. "We didn't have a meeting booked, did we?"

"No, we did not, Sanella," she said in an electric voice. Grandmama walked over to the chair and sat down. I sat beside her, a rage bubbling deep inside me. There was nothing more I wanted than to rip shreds into the man, but this was Farrah's rodeo, and I would not interfere with the sweet justice she was about to serve.

It was Farrah's tone that was enough to pull his attention

from whatever was on his screen to her. "Have I taken care of you, Sanella?"

He adjusted in his chair. "Yes, of course."

"Tell me something. Why would you steal from me then?"

His eyes widened, flickering from me to Farrah. "I don't know what you're talking about."

The asshole was trying to hide it? I should have known.

"I see."

Grandmama turned to face me. "What was it, Aristotle?"

"Four million three hundred and thirty-three thousand dollars, with most of that in the last four months." I stared at him with a vengeful look in my eyes.

How dare he do something like that to the woman who had worked so hard all of her life. I gripped the seat. My skin stretched painfully at the force.

"Did you think we wouldn't find out?" Farrah asked, her voice deathly calm.

How was she so calm when I was an explosion ready to erupt?

"You have no proof," he countered, his hand lifted to his neck, loosening the collar of his shirt.

"On the contrary. We have all the proof we need. Aristotle here has already handed it over to the police, and they are in the foyer."

He stood up, the force rolling his chair back so it hit the wall. Immediately, I did the same.

"Why? You want to know why? Because I knew one day Ari would be back, and you would give it all to him. Everything I have and everything I did was for the betterment of this company. Because one day it would be mine." He slammed his fist against the table, baring his teeth.

"This company was never yours, Sanella." Grandmama stood. "This was always a family business. My business. From the ground up, I nurtured the seeds that made this brand one of the leading fashion houses in America. I remunerated you more than anyone else in this business."

I watched Sanella's face change from ghastly white to ruby red.

"That's bullshit!" he accused. "When Ari left, there was a hidden promise that one day this would be all mine."

"You're delusional," I said, knowing that Farrah would rather leave the company to someone in the family rather than an employee.

"How dare you come back here? Strolling in here like you're some Manhattan rich kid taking what's his."

"I don't care who Farrah leaves this company to, as long as it's not you," I said, pointing my finger at him.

"Spoiled, ungrateful…"

"Stop right there, Sanella. Ari isn't any of those things, and I won't let you speak to him like that."

I turned to my grandmama, her loyalty warming but unnecessary because my rage filled my chest, and right now, I was about to get the guy by the shirt and throw him out of the building if he continued.

"Pretty boy can't defend himself?"

I laughed, but the rage bubbled inside me, growing uncontrollable by the second.

"I suggest you stay on that side of the desk, Sanella, if you know what's good for you."

He let out a loud cackle, spit landing on his desk. "Maybe if you hadn't killed your fiancé, we wouldn't be in this situation."

My veins flushed cold, and suddenly, my legs moved from beneath me. Quicker than a flash, I launched across the desk, kicking his computer to the floor, then landed on the other side of the desk and fisted him by the collar. His eyes widened with alarm, but I didn't care. I pushed him against the back wall, pinning him with my shoulder.

"Security! Security!" Grandmama screamed. "Ari, stop!" she yelled. But her words meant nothing. I wanted to hurt the man.

My hands fell around his neck, squeezing as tight as I could. I felt him struggle for air.

He tried moving, but I had him pinned down, my body against his, and the tighter I squeezed, the less he struggled until his eyes started rolling back in his head, and something inside me clicked. I jerked back, removing my hands and watching him as he gasped for air, taking his hands to his neck and sucking in oxygen.

I stepped back, hitting the desk, unsure who the monster was that just overtook me. Then the door swung open and detectives scrambled inside.

"He tried to kill me!" Sanella tried to scream out, but his voice was strained.

I felt Grandmama's hand on my shoulder.

"William Sanella, you are under arrest for alleged fraud and money laundering." A bald man with plain clothes grabbed him by the scruff of the neck and pinned him face down on the desk.

"You have the right to remain silent. Anything you say can and will be used against you in a court of law. You have the right to an attorney. If you cannot afford an attorney, one will be appointed for you. Do you understand these rights?"

Removing the handcuffs from his waist, he slammed on the metal chains as I tried to grapple with what had just transpired.

"Yes," Sanella hissed out.

After they led him away and Drummond from accounting, Grandmama said she would finish up with the detectives, purposely giving me space to calm down. But in that moment with Sanella, everything clicked—the rage, the anxiety, the guilt—it was as visceral as ever but instead of acting on it, like I usually did, I knew exactly what I had to do. It was the hardest thing I'd ever have to do in my life.

But finally, I was ready.

25

OLIVIA

When I got home, I was exhausted. The entire revamp was completed, but I was still on edge about tomorrow's launch.

I showered, changed, and was in the kitchen when I heard a fumbling at the front door. The door swung open, and Dario burst inside.

"I'm back, bitches," he said, pulling his suitcase behind him and shutting the door.

"Dario!" I ran round, and he pulled me in for a hug. A hug I needed. I gripped his shoulders and didn't let go.

"Well, someone missed me! Or was it my gourmet cooking you missed?"

I laughed, then let him go.

"Both. How was Italy?"

He breathed out a sigh. "Ah, the motherland. I miss it already. The women, the men, the lifestyle. I want it all!"

"The vino?" I asked.

"Oh, the vino. I did a tour in Tuscany, visiting vineyard after vineyard. The next morning I woke up with a terrible hangover and a guy to my right and a woman to my left."

I pushed him on the shoulder. "A woman? Venturing to the other side?"

"We do strange things when we're drunk… but give me a dick any day of the week."

I laughed aloud, then grabbed him by the hand. "Come, I want to hear all about it. It will get my mind off the last couple of weeks I've had."

I pulled him over to the kitchen, grabbed a bag of nuts, and tore the packet open. Then fetching two glasses and a bottle of red wine, I plopped on the seat beside him and poured us each a glass.

"It's almost a travesty having this wine, but I'm jetlagged as fuck, so I'll drink it." We clinked glasses, and I downed the wine. It tasted like wine to me. Anything to numb the pain and take the edge off was good enough for me.

I watched him screw his face up as he swallowed the All-American wine from the local liquor store. "Ghastly."

"Feel free to buy something else," I said, pouring myself another after quickly downing the first.

"Wait, tell me about you. What's going on? You saw all my social media updates. My trip can wait. I know you, girl, and something is on your mind."

I looked down, trying to avoid the turmoil in my heart.

"I've got my biggest day ever tomorrow, and I'm so screwed. I can't stop thinking about my boss, who is Ari Goldsmith, by the way."

He gasped. "*The* Ari? The same Ari you've been locking horns with who's friends with Lourde?"

"True story."

"Why didn't you tell me?"

"You were going away. I didn't want to burden you with my problems."

"You fucked him, didn't you?"

I nodded, sucking down the wine in gallons so I didn't have to talk.

"You bad girl. Was he good? Are the rumors true about his cock being the size of the spire at the top of the Empire State Building?"

I nearly spat out my wine. "Dario, this is not funny…"

He shrieked as his hand touched the tip of his nose. "Oh my God, it is. The man's hung like a horse, isn't he?"

I smiled, and damn, it was good to have my roommate back.

"You lucky girl."

"Well, no," I said, picking up a piece of invisible lint off my pants.

"It's complicated. We aren't together. I'm not sure if we were ever really together. But I can't stop thinking about him, even though I know he isn't what I should want, I do, and I can't reconcile that in my analytical mind."

"Girl, maybe you should stop thinking with that big brain of yours for once."

I shook my head. "He doesn't want me, anyway. It doesn't matter."

"As if he wouldn't want you? Are you crazy?"

"I'm no model. I'm not what he wants. I don't cower to his every whim. We fight, we challenge each other. It's not easy."

"Is that a bad thing? Maybe he doesn't want a model to sit on his knee all day long and suck his delicious dick dry."

I put my head in my hands. "Dario, please!" The image made me insanely jealous, and nausea formed in the base of my belly.

"All I'm saying is, maybe he's looking for something more. And that something more is you, Liv." He pulled out his hand and put it in mine, lifting it from my face.

"I think the timing is wrong. We weren't meant to be."

"Well, we need to show him exactly what he's missing out on then."

"What are you talking about?"

"Let's drink and get crazy drunk. That way, I can get over my jet lag and be your date tomorrow at the store opening."

I thought about it for a moment. It wasn't a good idea. "Yeah, nah."

"Don't wimp out on me. Grab your balls. and let's do this." Dario topped up both our glasses.

"There will be gorgeous male models there, and we can make Mr. Ari insanely jealous."

I guess I didn't have to work tomorrow, but just show up, and there would be a thousand models there so…

"Oh, heck, why not?" I picked up the glass and clicked it with his.

"Yes, that's my girl."

"To getting drunk and getting dick," he cheered, gulping down the wine.

I laughed, then drank down the remaining wine, feeling the sweetness sliding down the back of my throat. I knew deep down that bringing Dario as my date to a work event wasn't a good idea. But I was lost, needing to get over my heartache of Ari but unsure how. So it was all or nothing.

26

ARI

Riding along the highway, I took the turnoff to Rookburn Cemetery. It was after ten at night when I decided to go and see her. I hadn't been to Sophia's resting place for a very long time, wanting to avoid the pain as much as possible. But even after today's events and the events that had transpired over the last three weeks with Olivia, all roads led to here.

And as I pulled off the road into the empty parking spot, I shut off the engine and rested my hands on the steering wheel. Tapping them like a cartwheel on the wheel, I hesitated. But I was left with zero options, and I had to make my peace. Time spent with Olivia made me realize I wasn't living. I was barely existing at best. And if that weren't enough, I could have killed Sanella this afternoon with my bare hands.

And for what? Fraud? No, it was way more than that. My rage had nothing to do with Sanella and everything to do with me not facing my own demons.

My hands slid down the wheel, and reluctantly, I pushed open the car door, taking the flowers with me. Shutting it behind me, I leaned against the Maserati. A light above the parking lot lit up a nearby pathway that led to the cemetery entrance.

I didn't need the light to lead me. I knew exactly where she was buried.

Where *they* were buried.

With my legs like lead, I willed myself to move from the car. I walked along the cobbled pathway, heavy legs propelling me forward with each step. I passed headstones and crypts until finally, I reached her.

A faint light nearby lit up the headstone, and I stood at the foot of it. Bowing my head, I placed the flowers at the foot of her grave. Her favorite. Peonies.

Sadness washed over me as I remembered her smile and the last fleeting look she gave me before the accident.

I fell to my knees, moist dirt soaked through my trousers. The air was still, the trees were statues, and the scent was floral from the nearby gardens.

"Angel, I'm sorry," I whispered. "I miss you every day." I lifted the dirt beneath my fingers, wanting to feel her.

With my head bowed, I let the emotion overcome me. "I miss you both," I said.

When I looked up, I settled my gaze on the butterfly I had engraved just below her name. A butterfly represented the life growing inside her, the five-week-old embryo that perished along with her.

The baby who could have been ours.

"Sophia, I can't do this anymore. I can't live like this."

"Tell me it's okay to move on, to forgive myself. Because I love her. "

I held her headstone in both my hands as emotion overwhelmed me.

"I love Olivia with everything I am. And that doesn't mean I love you any less. I just have to let you go. I deserve to be happy, and Olivia makes me happy. She has brought light back after the darkness that was left in my world after you were gone. The darkness that swallowed me whole and nearly consumed me."

I let my head hit the cool stone of her headstone and closed my eyes. When I opened them, I took in a lungful of crisp air.

"I need to let you both go," I admitted, tracing the butterfly.

When I finally stood, I didn't know how much time had passed.

"Give me something, please, Sophia, I beg you."

I shook my head. I didn't know what I was doing, asking her, but I waited there and just when I was about to turn back to the car, it happened. In the distance, an owl hooting echoed through the trees down the valley. It was crystal clear.

Desperately, I glanced around, trying to find it. Then it sounded again. This time, it was closer. Immediately, my gaze set to the nearby tree where I heard the noise. And there, in clear view on an overhanging branch, was a barn owl staring straight at me. It was the signal I'd been waiting for.

Again, it hooted as I stared at it. I was lost for words.

I turned to the headstone, "I hear you, Sophia." This time the owl continued hoot after hoot, and something inside me shifted. I rested my hands on the headstone and kissed it.

"I will never forget you," I said, and with that, I turned and walked across the cobblestone pathway, the owl still hooting in the distance, bringing me the peace internally that I'd craved for a decade.

* * *

It was the morning of the store opening, and I decided to message her. Unsure what to say, I just hoped for the best.

Me: *Excited about this evening?*

But with no reply, I busied myself all day until my phone pinged when I was putting on my tuxedo jacket and about to head out the door.

Olivia: *Yes.*

Her reply was curt, and I quickly thumbed out a response.

Me: *I can't wait to see you.*

I waited patiently for a reply.

Nothing. Nil. It was approaching seven, and staring at my phone was causing me more anxiety, especially as I didn't want to keep my grandmama waiting.

I grabbed my wallet and met the driver downstairs.

My driver opened the door and Farrah was inside.

"Grandmama, wasn't I picking you up?" I asked, confused to see her in the back seat.

"I thought I'd surprise you."

I slid inside the car and kissed her on both cheeks.

"You look fabulous as always," I said, admiring her signature gown. Lilac and floor length, she looked every bit the matriarch of the fashion world and not a hint of her eighty-three years of age.

"I know." She let out a chuckle and pinched her cheeks so they appeared red.

She put her hand on my knee as the driver shut his door, and the car slid forward.

"And you are handsome, Aristotle, inside and out."

"Thanks, Grandmama. We make a good team, don't we?" I admired everything this lady had done for me in my life. As I looked out at passing cars, she had always been there when my parents were away traveling. She had taught me so much more than them, and I wouldn't be the man I was today without her.

Giving me a place to work when I couldn't be bothered, she was the driving force behind me to get better, and without her, I honestly don't know where I'd be.

"What happened yesterday?" she asked, her voice floating inside the car. Soft and caring, she squeezed my hand in hers.

"Everything just came to a head, and Sanella seemed like the appropriate object of my anger."

"I don't blame you, the guy is a jerk, and with all the evidence you and your team have gathered on him, he will be put away for a very long time."

"Good," I said.

"Are you okay now?"

"Yes, I'm perfect. I went to see her."

"Olivia?"

"No." I turned to face her. "I went to see Sophia."

Her eyes widened. "Excellent."

"Excellent?" I responded, confused.

"It's about damn time."

"Grandmama?" I furrowed my brow.

"For years, I've wanted you to see her. To get the closure you needed."

"I wasn't ready," I shared, and it was the truth.

"Did you get what you needed?"

"Yes, I did," I said, sucking in a breath. "I let them both go."

Grandmama looked at me with glassy eyes. She was the only other person who knew Sophia was pregnant at the time. She was the only other person I could tell.

She put her hand on my knee. "Oh, Ari, I'm so proud of you."

I smiled back at her, for once proud of myself too for mustering the courage to visit her.

The car pulled to a halt, and I looked outside. "We're here," I said, staring up at the bright lights and crowd.

"Oh, blooming hell. Tell the driver to go around the block. I look like a train wreck."

"Marcel, a lap, please," I said, tapping on the glass divider between us.

She pulled out a tissue and dabbed below her eyes.

"You look amazing, Grandmama."

"Only family can say that!" She patted my shoulder. "Now, are you ready to go and get your girl?"

"Hell, yes," I replied. There was a fire that burned inside me for the woman who had captured my heart and thrown away the key.

"Okay, we're ready, Marcel," she said, straightening her shoulders and lengthening her curved back.

My mannerisms mirrored hers. The apple didn't fall too far from the tree. I laughed as she looked at me. "The world is yours, Aristotle. Take it."

The car stopped, and our door opened. I leaped out first, helping my grandmama out. We stood, waving and smiling at flashing bulbs and paparazzi.

Red carpet lay at our feet, and as I looped my arm in Grandmama's, we walked toward the front doors.

Fashionably late, of course, hundreds of people were already inside—the industry's best and brightest with the best ticket in town. As the crowd parted, a woman wearing a backless gown stole my breath away. I had committed the curves of her body to memory, and it was like slow motion as she turned. Her eyes locked on mine, and the breath escaped my lungs.

Her beauty was a sin, and the tension between us exploded like fireworks. But then the crowd parted more, and I saw a man beside her, a hand pulling around her waist as she pulled him tighter.

I stopped, unsure of what was happening. Rage shot through my chest like an arrow to a bullseye.

Who the fuck was the man touching my girl?

I made my way toward them both with a purpose in my step.

27

OLIVIA

Even with the discount, it was still a lot of money. I'd treated myself and shelled out on one of Farrah's own couture dresses. It helped when she offered staff and suppliers a hefty discount, and so why not? But today, I was experiencing some post-purchase remorse.

Mind you. I had committed to the purchase after our third bottle of vino last night and organized an Uber to send it to me this morning from work.

"Darling, he's not going to know what hit him, fuck the models. You are magnificent," he stated, staring at me from head to toe and giving me a knowing nod.

Surprised at how well Farrah's dress fit me, I admired myself in the mirror before getting into the waiting Uber. The floor-length backless dress fitting like a glove showed off my curves and decolletage. And coupled with my heels and a pop of red lipstick, the dress transformed me completely.

But not my nerves.

They remained.

I gripped Dario for support as we got out of the Uber and into the waiting paparazzi.

"Holy smokes, this is gorg!" Dario said as we approached the front doors. I quickly scanned the crowd for Ari, but he wasn't there. *Great.* Perhaps I could avoid him altogether.

I mean, what was the deal with his text this afternoon? Were we friends now?

I shook my head just as a reporter shoved a microphone into my face and a blaring light.

"Olivia, do you have a moment?"

"Ah." I held onto Dario, uncertain how a reporter knew my name.

"Of course, she does," Dario exclaimed, stopping us both so I could have a chat.

"This store is amazing. Tell me, is the collaboration with you and Farrah Goldsmith going to continue?"

I laughed nervously. Truth was, Farrah had mentioned all her stores on the East Coast at the outset of our contract, and now this one was ending, I was hesitant. Not because I didn't love my job but because I needed a break from the emotions wreaking havoc in my heart.

"Nothing is out of the question," I said, smiling.

"Where do you draw your inspiration from? The colors and detail in here is like nothing I've ever seen before."

"I don't know to be honest. I have these ideas in my head that jump out at me. There is really no stopping them!"

"Well, it is just exquisite. Can we have a picture, please, for the article?"

"Sure," I said, holding onto Dario.

The photographer snapped away, then took one look at Dario, then me. "And one alone, please."

"Oh, right."

"Turn around and look over your shoulder," Dario suggested to my horror. "That dress is too hot not to be pictured that way."

The reporter laughed, and as I turned, she nodded in agreement. "Absolutely, that is stunning."

I looked over my shoulder, my back to the camera, and I smiled slightly, feeling like everyone else here posing. Except it came so unnaturally to me.

"Perfect. Now just confirming the name of your business is Bespoke Interiors?"

"Yes, with my partner and friend, Lourde Diamond."

She jotted down the name.

"Soon, you'll never have to ask again," Dario pointed out and looped his arm in mine, whisking me away to the lights and fanfare ahead of us.

"I'm glad that's over with," I said nervously, looking around and pulling a strand of loose hair off my face.

"Would you stop? You look fabulous!"

But nerves knocked against the walls of my empty stomach. "This wasn't a good idea, Dario, you being here."

"I think it was my best idea yet," he exclaimed. "Anyway, there's no backing out now because here's your boy."

"He's not my boy," I said, snatching a glass of champagne off a waiter's tray and gulping it down.

Through the crowd, I saw him, but he hadn't seen me. Dressed in a tuxedo, holding his grandmama, it was hard to think this was the same man I fought with so often. His hair to one side, shoulders straight and jaw strong, he had this commanding presence that took me aback. Paparazzi swarmed with flashing lights and microphones.

I swallowed down the emotion and the fire in my loins. Instead, I turned around, not wanting to face him. Sensing my discomfort, Dario's hand fell around my waist, then pulling me closer, he whispered, "Trust me, everything will be just fine."

Nerves filled me from head to toe, and after a deep breath, I turned around slowly. His eyes immediately connected with mine, and it was like time stood still. Something passed between us that filled my belly and lit a fire inside me.

A thousand-yard stare still had the same impact it did, as if he were standing a breadth away from me. But as the crowd parted to let them walk through, he stopped. His jaw tightened, his back like an arrow. Something was wrong, and I knew exactly what.

"Someone's jealous," Dario whispered in my ear, pulling me closer, and my heart beat erratically in my chest.

"Just smile, Livvy. You've got this, babe."

"I've got this," I echoed, and a smile lifted onto my scarlet lips. "Let's mingle," I said, wanting to avoid him at all costs. "I think I saw Lourde and Barrett and Pepper and Connor upstairs. Let's go say hello."

"Oh fabulous, I've always wanted to meet those two hunky boys."

We walked around to the front of the spiral staircase, and holding onto the rail, I carefully navigated each step, making sure I didn't fall flat on my face.

"You know they're not gay, right?" I questioned, my gaze momentarily pulling from the staircase and down to the entrance. There, brown eyes stared up at me. Fear exploded inside me, but I held it together, barely composed but damn sure not to let him see that.

He was the one who pulled away after chasing me. He was the one who went completely AWOL on the jet from Vegas to home, then made zero attempts to make things right between us.

I lifted my head high and ignored his penetrating stare.

"A man can dream," Dario said on a sigh. "Anyway, I need to meet these new friends of yours because you've been spending way too much time with them and not me!"

When I turned to Dario, his lips were pouty in an attempt to make me feel bad.

"Hello, you have been in Italy!"

He flapped his spare hand about. "Yes, well." He laughed, and when we reached the top step, I was relieved to be there, putting space between Ari and me.

"There she is!" Pepper and Lourde came over to hug me. "This is amazing," Pepper said.

Lourde looked stunning in a red dress with a fishtail skirt that clung to her hips. "Morning sickness is a bitch," she whispered.

"Oh, hun, well, you look gorgeous if that's any consolation."

"Hello, look who is smashing herself!"

"Isn't she just," Dario interjected.

"So this must be the elusive Dario. You know, I thought he didn't exist!" Pepper said, kissing him on each cheek.

"How do you know?"

"You texted us last night saying you're bringing him. You don't remember?" Lourde looked at me with a strange expression.

Perplexed, I looked at Dario, and he laughed. "Honey, we had a blinder last night, and my head is still in the clouds from jet lag. I don't remember a thang," he said. "But so nice to meet you!" He pulled Lourde and Pepper in for a squeezy hug.

"Okay! Too much?" he said, releasing them, and we all laughed.

"Connor and Barrett are wondering who this handsome man is that just touched their missuses," he said, pulling his face into an uncertain frown.

"Maybe you should introduce yourself then?" Pepper said, and I could tell they wanted some alone time with me.

What else had I texted them last night? Shit, my memory was so fuzzy.

A waiter came by with a tray of hors d'oeuvres. "Salmon and caviar on a wafer?"

Lourde paled.

"No, please take it away," I said.

The waiter did as he was told and retreated.

"Are you okay?" I asked.

"Morning sickness truly sucks."

"What, you have it now at nighttime?"

"It doesn't matter what time it is. It comes wherever it fucking well wants," she complained.

"That's what you get for sleeping with your fiancé all the damn time," Pepper said. "You know, Olivia, I walked in on them the other day." She shook her head at the memory. "Oh. My. God."

Lourde and I both laughed.

"Look, Dario is actually introducing himself," Pepper said in disbelief.

"He seems like fun in a bucket," Lourde said.

"He is. He is also my anchor tonight," I admitted, missing his support.

"You do seem rather nervous," Lourde remarked.

"It's a big night," I exclaimed. "I'm hoping Farrah sells out and we get rave reviews on the revamp."

"The new store is lit. Once I get over this morning sickness, I'm back on board to help. Has she confirmed the East Coast contract for the other stores?"

"Oh…" I sighed. "Yeah, I'm not sure about that."

"You're not going to let what happened between you and Ari influence the business, are you?"

Damn, what did I text them?

"You don't remember what you sent us on Messenger, do you?" Pepper raised her perfectly plucked brows.

I shook my head. "No, no idea."

Pepper pulled out her phone from her Balenciaga clutch and clicked on the chat between the three of us. Immediately I took it from her and read the messages.

Olivia: *How could he just desert me like we never existed?*
Pepper: *Hun, I feel you.*
Lourde: *Maybe he's going through something...*
Olivia: *Come on, we all have shit to deal with. One minute he wants me the next, he doesn't. I opened up to him, and he crushed my heart.*
Olivia: *I love him, you know.*
Olivia: *No. I hate him. I loathe him. How could he do this to me?*
Pepper: *You love him?*
Lourde: *How much have you had to drink?*
Lourde: *Do you need us to come over?*
Lourde: *?*
Olivia: *I'm finnnee! Dario is here. He is back from Italy and yes, we are drinking... a lot but so what? I'm bringing him tomorrow as my date, so screw Ari. I hope he is happy fucking models for the rest of his life.*
Lourde: *Sending hugs and have a vino for me while I sit here throwing up absolutely nothing!*
Pepper: *Gross. Liv, sleep it off. Tomorrow is a new day.*

I gazed up in horror. And they stared back at me. "I drank way too much last night."

"You think?" Pepper said, thrusting her hand on her hip.

"Girl, you did me a solid on the one drink," Lourde said, chuckling.

"I did way more than that. Way more."

"Well, while you were drinking with cute Dario over there, I think I had the most orgasms in one evening ever," Pepper shared and looked over at Connor. At the same time, he looked at her, a knowing smile on his face.

"Oh my, can you not? That's my brother, and I swear I'll vomit right here making a mess of this lush herringbone floor."

I laughed out loud.

"Okay, too much?" Pepper inquired, giggling.

"Way. Too. Much." Lourde reached for a glass of water

from the nearby waiter and sipped it, then cleared her throat, composing herself.

The moment of pause allowed me to scour the crowd as music washed over the gorgeous people. Everyone was having the best time, and Farrah, who I should probably be saying hello to, was mingling and looking like she was right at home and in her element.

But I couldn't see him.

"Looking for Ari?" Lourde asked, making her way back over.

"No." I straightened and caught Pepper and Lourde eyeing me with curiosity. "Well, okay, maybe. Anyway, he's probably with a harem of models doing what he does best."

"Flirt and womanize?" Pepper added.

"Exactly."

"Guys, you know he only became that way after Sophia died, right?"

"Who?" Pepper asked.

"Wait. you don't know?" Lourde said.

"I know," I admitted, but I didn't know she knew. Anyway, none of it mattered now. He had quit on me the first opportunity he had.

"Ari was engaged when he was twenty-three. In a tragic twist of events, they were traveling home from a vacation together when the car hit some bad weather and hydroplaned off the road, hitting a tree." Lourde looked up at me.

"She died," I added. "It is so very sad," I said, sucking in a breath.

"Shit, I had no idea," Pepper said. "Ari? Ari was engaged?"

"I know it came as a shock to me too, at first," I admitted.

"I think you changed him, Olivia. Ari and Connor have been friends for a long time, and I have known Ari for over a decade. I haven't seen him as happy as the time he was with you in Vegas."

I shook my head and held onto the rail, wrapping my hand around the smooth timber. It gave me the support I needed when Dario wasn't here. "It was fun while it lasted, but nothing lasts forever."

"You can't mean that," Lourde said.

"I do." I cleared my throat, "Anyway, I'm going off to fetch Dario before he tries to convert Barrett and Connor to his team. Chat later?"

"Oh, please do!" Pepper said, laughing.

Lourde stared at me, knowing exactly what I was doing. Avoiding an uncomfortable situation was my middle name, and talking about my feelings wasn't something I did, and this was becoming very uncomfortable.

"Go, but you can't avoid him or me forever," she yelled out into the crowd, causing others to turn their heads and look.

I glanced around the top floor, but none of the eyes on me were those of Ari's familiar soothing brown eyes.

"Darling, Connor and Barrett were just telling me about your working conditions with Ari," Dario said. "Why didn't you tell me he was such a jerk face to you? I would have flown right back and slapped some sense into him."

"I tried," Barrett interjected. "To talk some sense into him."

"I didn't tell you, Barrett. How did you…" I paused then the penny dropped. "Lourde."

"Of course, she told me. Well, in all honesty, I dragged it out of her. You don't want to know how." A glint of a smile peeled onto his mouth.

"Well, it doesn't matter. He could argue I was also a bitch. So…" I shrugged my shoulders, leaving the sentence in the balance as my gaze fell to the floor. When I looked back up, I had three sets of eyes on me.

"What?" I asked.

Missing Love

"You've fallen for Ari, haven't you?" Barrett asked, scratching his forehead.

Damn.

I know. The truth was a very odd reality to face.

"Maybe for a while there, sure, I let myself go. But it didn't work out. I'm not want he wants, and I'm just too busy starting this new business to let myself get caught up in a relationship."

"Right," Connor said, rolling his eyes.

"Look at this place, though. Hasn't my girl outdone herself?" Dario threw around his hands in admiration. "After this, she will be so busy. Soon she will say, Ari, who?"

I gazed around. The store opening was a roaring success. A live band played against the backdrop of beautiful people sipping vintage Cristal and whiskey and admiring the expensive, exquisite pieces of couture on the racks.

This was what I'd wanted. My own success and freedom. With that came the ability to fast-track my parents' loan repayments with any extra money I had put across to pay down their debt. And with my help, and in less than a year, the house would be theirs, and they could live their lives in peace. Working this hard had gotten me this far, and standing here admiring what I had done was amazing, but something was missing.

I'd opened my heart up to Ari, and now that I had experienced the feeling of someone taking care of me, I wanted it back.

"It is a beauty, but I had no doubt you could pull it off, Olivia," Barrett said. Then his gaze drifted to behind me.

I felt him before I saw him.

The warmth of his body hit the exposed V of my back. It sent a flurry of warmth up my spine and around my shoulders and neck.

"Ari, my man," Connor said exuberantly. Ari stepped

beside me, his jacket brushing against my bare arm. I tilted my head down to the side.

He shook Connor and Barrett's hands and stopped and stared at Dario.

"And you are?"

"Dario, Olivia's date." Dario straightened, and Ari exhaled loudly beside me. The hairs on my arms stood up.

Oh fuck.

Connor let out a laugh. "We'll catch up with you all later," Barrett said, grabbing his glass of whiskey from the nearby table. Then he and Connor walked off, leaving the three of us alone.

When I lifted my head, Ari was already staring at me. His eyes were dark and intense.

If anyone ought to be angry, it was me. How could Ari be jealous when he was the one who was hot one minute, then colder than ice the next? I straightened, not letting him affect me.

"I need to talk to you," he said, his voice barely controlled.

"You want to talk now? Here?" I shook my head. "I don't think so, Ari."

Dario came to my side and pulled his arm around my waist.

Ari's eyes widened, and his jaw ticked.

"I don't care who this is, Olivia. But if you don't come with me now…"

"You'll what?" Dario interjected. Pulling me close, his hand lingered on my hip in a gesture certain to infuriate Ari even more.

Ari's gaze dropped to my waist. When his eyes came back up to mine, a fire burned behind them. "Do you want me to fight for you? Is that it? Because I will, Olivia, I will fight to the death, starting with this asshole first."

"Asshole?" Dario let go of my waist. "You had your chance, and you blew it."

I stood there, unable to contemplate the exchange going on between the two of them.

I couldn't understand it. I was so angry with Ari. Dario was just trying to protect me.

As their voices reached a higher decibel, heads turned in our direction.

"You know nothing about us." He stepped closer to Dario, then turned toward me. "Olivia..." His hand fell around my arm, and he pulled me toward him. His warmth felt reassuring and safe until I remembered how in an instant, he'd offered me that before, then it was gone. He had turned whatever he felt about us off and left me a blithering mess because of it. Well, forget it, I wouldn't be his fool twice.

Dario pulled me back toward him, and suddenly, I was the one feeling like a ping-pong ball being passed from player to player.

"Enough," I whispered out in force and stepped out of both of their grasps.

Ari looked at me, surprised by my reaction.

"He's right. You had your chance, Ari. You call me the Ice Queen? Well, you were colder than that after Vegas. I told you before. We're done. Now leave me alone."

A vulnerability in his mocha eyes hit me squarely in the chest and had my emotions threatening to spill over. No, that would not be me. Before it could take hold, I quickly brushed past them, almost knocking into Lourde on the way to the stairwell.

"Olivia, stop!" Lourde pleaded with me, but I burst past her like a hurricane, feigning my best fake smile. Instead, I gripped the handrail and descended the staircase as quickly as I could but without causing a scene.

Without looking back, I hurried past the crowds of beautiful people, oblivious to my aching heart, and exited the glass front doors to the Manhattan sidewalk.

With the paparazzi inside, I was able to release the breath I'd been holding in. But what happened next threw me. My eyes glazed with unshed tears as emotion clawed at me, suffocating me from the neck up. I had to get out of here, but I didn't want to go home.

I recognized Ari's driver with the car out front, but I avoided him. I saw the taxi rank across the road, and as tears began to fall, I quickened my pace, trying to avoid being seen.

I opened the back door. "Just drive," I blurted out as tears fell, and the floodgates opened.

28

ARI

It had been more than twenty-four hours since Olivia ran out on me.

Her words cut like a shark bite, and the moment I stood there processing what she had said was a moment too long. Because when I took the stairs two at a time to go after her, she was gone.

Then the paparazzi swarmed around me, asking questions. Questions they had no business asking.

* * *

The concierge held open the glass doors, and I walked outside. The sun was out with not a cloud in the sky, but I wasn't cheery.

My driver greeted me, and I barely acknowledged him. I slid into the back of the car and pulled out my phone again. Nothing. Not one call had she returned. Not one text. She'd gone MIA, and I mean completely MIA, not even her roommate. Yes, fucking Dario, who I was told was batting for the other team, had not heard from her.

She hadn't returned home, nor had she phoned any of us since the launch.

Lourde and Pepper were worried sick, thinking someone had kidnapped her. I just missed my girl.

But she wasn't mine anymore. I'd completely blown it.

I threw my phone against the back seat, the force hitting the side of the door.

I put my head in my hands, and when I looked up, my driver was staring at me.

"Sir, I hope you don't mind me saying, but I saw Olivia after the party. She stepped into a taxi looking so distraught."

"What?"

"I don't know why, but I took down the taxi's details."

Hope sprung into my chest. "Pullover," I said.

A few moments later, I was on the phone with the taxi company.

"Yes, I remember her. She was so sad."

My ribcage squeezed together.

"Where did you take her," I asked.

"I'm not supposed to tell you."

"Just fucking tell me," I said desperately.

"Okay, man, relax. The truth is, I can't really tell you because we were on the highway northbound to Connecticut. We made one stop at a gas station where she picked up some supplies, then we kept travelling north. All of a sudden, she's asking me to pull over to the side of the road. We were in the middle of nowhere."

The barn.

She had to be there, and there was only one way to find out.

"Thanks, man," I said and clicked off the phone.

"I need the car. Take the day off," I said to my driver.

* * *

For two hours, I'd been driving when I pulled up to the abandoned barn just past Redding.

I had rehearsed what I would say to her a thousand times over on the drive, but when I ran through the wild grasses toward her, the only thing I could hear was my pounding heart.

I pushed the splintered door open, and Olivia turned, startled at the noise. Wearing no makeup and sweats, she looked every bit like my girl.

I breathed out a sigh of relief.

"What on earth, Ari…"

I took a moment to suck in a few breaths. Memories of us making love on the blanket beside where she now sat burned into my memory.

"I will not make this a memory," I said, stepping closer toward her.

"Did you bump your head or something?" she asked, closing the book she was reading and standing.

"I will not make what we did on this floor, with the stars above us, a memory, Olivia."

She rolled her lips on in themselves. "Well, I have. You've wasted your time coming here. I said what I had to say at the party."

"We're done," I repeated her words. "I heard you."

"Fabulous. So now you can go on home…" She went to turn around and dropped her book instead, sending dust particles in the air.

I walked over, picked it up, and handed it to her. God, I missed her smell. "Austen?"

She shrugged. "I didn't think a murder mystery would be a good first choice, considering my location."

"I think Austen was your first choice."

She blinked but didn't argue back. "I also know that Dario

is your roommate and that little stunt you both pulled to make me insanely jealous worked."

She shook her head, her gaze falling to the ground. "That was his idea."

"Olivia, I need to tell you why I reacted that way on the plane."

"No, you don't," she said, shaking her head.

I reached for her arm and pulled her close. "Let me explain, please. If then you want me to go, I will."

"You drove all this way for a simple conversation."

"Well, if you had picked up your damn phone…"

"Ugh! You are so infuriating. Fine, tell me," she bit out, but she didn't move away from my grasp. I left my hand on hers, stroking her arm gently as I inhaled.

"Lourde and Barrett announcing the news they were pregnant was upsetting, to say the very least."

"Why? Shouldn't you be happy for them? We were all so happy."

"Sophia was five weeks pregnant at the time of the accident. I not only lost her but our baby too."

Immediately her hand fell around mine. "Oh, Ari, I'm so sorry."

"I just couldn't deal with the news and pushed you away, Olivia."

She blinked back the tears that glazed over her indigo eyes.

"I regret it. The piece of my life that has been missing is you. "I raked a hand through my hair, unsure if any of this was registering with her. "You were the last person I thought would make me feel the way I do about you."

"Ari, honestly, I just think it's better if we remain friends."

"Let me take care of you, Olivia. Let me love you like you deserve to be loved."

She tilted her head down. I held her chin in my hands, my thumb stroking her jaw, then lifted her head, forcing her to look at me. When she did, a tear escaped from the corner of her eye.

"I don't think I can take it," she whispered.

"You're my Ice Queen, princess. You can take everything."

She choked out a laugh.

"And I'm crazy in love with you, Ms. Willows."

Olivia let out a cry, and I swallowed the sound with a kiss. Immediately, she parted her lips and let me in. I gripped the sides of her face and kissed her like it was the first day of forever.

Her arms lifted to my shoulders, gripping onto my arms.

She moaned into my mouth, wrapping her hands around the nape of my neck as she stood on her toes. Our tongues clashed together as our bodies pressed firmly against one another. My kiss turned possessive as she shifted her hold and gripped my forearms, her nails digging in.

She pulled back, breathless. "You win, Ari Goldsmith. I'm yours."

I smiled, every cell in my body screaming with happiness.

Her hands clawed down the front of my chest, then down to the bulge pressing against my zipper. She squeezed my balls gently, and I panicked momentarily. "But if you hurt me again, you're history."

A smirk left her lips and damn.

She was the fucking stars.

THE END

ALSO BY MISSY WALKER

Sassy Seaview Series

Trusting a Rockstar

Return to Home

Beyond Melting

Elite Men of Manhattan Series

Forbidden Lust

Forbidden Love

Lost Love

Missing Love

Fairbank Series

(coming soon)

Unloveable #1

Untangled #2

Join Missy's Club

Hear about exclusive book releases, teasers and box sets before anyone else.

Sign up to her newsletter here:
www.authormissywalker.com

Become part of Missy's Facebook Crew
www.facebook.com/AuthorMissyWalker

ACKNOWLEDGMENTS

To my beta readers, Gemma, Stacey and Maria. A massive thank you, your suggestions are as always on point and perfect.

To my fellow indie authors. Being an author can be a lonely road if you let it. We do it all, working tirelessly from writing to marketing to admin.

I've already made so many great friends in the book world and look forward to making so many more in this amazing community. Thank you for the advice, endless support, and the many writing sprints!

You know who you are.

Missy xx

ABOUT THE AUTHOR

Missy is an Australian author who writes kissing books with equal parts angst and steam. Stories about billionaires, forbidden romance, and second chances roll around in her mind probably more than they ought to.

When she's not writing, she's taking care of her two daughters and doting husband and conjuring up her next saucy plot.

Inspired by the acreage she lives on, Missy regularly distracts herself by visiting her orchard, baking naughty but delicious foods, and socialising with her girl squad.

Then there's her overweight cat Charlie, chickens, rabbit and bees if she needed another excuse to pass the time.

If you like Missy Walker's books, consider leaving a review and following her here:

tiktok.com/@authormissywalker
instagram.com/missywalkerauthor
facebook.com/AuthorMissyWalker
www.amazon.com/Missy-Walker
bookbub.com/profile/missy-walker

Printed in Great Britain
by Amazon